"DID YOU REALLY THINK I'D BE PUT OFF BY SOME HALF-BAKED SCHEME?" HE CHALLENGED. . . .

"Did you think I'd simply give up and slink off like some docile puppy?"

"I'd hardly classify you as docile," Adrian murmured. "As to the rest, I have a feeling all this is old hat to you."

"Ah, now I understand," he smiled. "You think I want a quick tumble and then good-bye. Right?"

"Crudely put, but true. And, in spite of your opinion, I do love Jason."

"You do believe in tempting fate, don't you, Adrian?" he whispered as he reached for her. The muscles in his face were taut. Suddenly there was a brilliant fire in his eyes. Adrian braced herself for the first moment of contact, thinking of how she might protect herself. But any protection she may have constructed was swept away like a fragile flower being swamped by a tidal wave.

A CANDLELIGHT ECSTASY ROMANCE ®

SENSUOUS PERSUASION

Eleanor Woods

A CANDLELIGHT ECSTASY ROMANCE ®

Published by
Dell Publishing Co., Inc.
1 Dag Hammarskjold Plaza
New York, New York 10017

Dell ® TM 681510, Dell Publishing Co., Inc.
Candlelight Ecstasy Romance®, 1,203,540, is a registered
trademark of Dell Publishing Co., Inc.,
New York, New York.

ISBN: 0–440–17954–8

Printed in the United States of America
First printing—December 1983

To Our Readers:

We have been delighted with your enthusiastic response to Candlelight Ecstasy Romances®, and we thank you for the interest you have shown in this exciting series.

In the upcoming months we will continue to present the distinctive sensuous love stories you have come to expect only from Ecstasy. We look forward to bringing you many more books from your favorite authors and also the very finest work from new authors of contemporary romantic fiction.

As always, we are striving to present the unique, absorbing love stories that you enjoy most—books that are more than ordinary romance.

Your suggestions and comments are always welcome. Please write to us at the address below.

Sincerely,

The Editors
Candlelight Romances
1 Dag Hammarskjold Plaza
New York, New York 10017

CHAPTER ONE

Adrian Kohl sat at her desk, the receiver braced against her ear by one shoulder, as she jotted down the particulars for the temporary opening of a cashier's position in one of the local restaurants.

Dan Colson had used the Kohl Agency a number of times and was now one of its steadiest customers.

"I believe I have the perfect young woman for you, Dan. Her name is Sally Lawrence. She's a student, but her schedule leaves her afternoons free. I'll have her at your place at twelve thirty tomorrow. Can you see her then?" Adrian asked.

"Twelve thirty sounds great, Adrian. If you think she's qualified, then I'm sure I'll be pleased," Dan replied.

After chatting for a few more minutes, Adrian cradled the receiver and leaned back in her chair, a pleased expression on her attractive face. For the last three years she'd driven herself unmercifully as she struggled to establish her small business and only lately had been able to breathe easily at the results.

Kohl Temps was exactly what its name implied, an employment agency that mainly offered temporary help to the various businesses in Savannah and to private citizens as well. Occasionally some of Adrian's "people" would find they liked whatever job they had been sent on, and would stay on permanently. Adrian found that other than having to add additional recruits to her list it gave added prestige to her firm, and insured a definite call for her services again.

The idea of having her own business had come about as a result of finding herself tied for four years to a boring job as secretary to the executive director of a large insurance company.

The risk factor involved in launching a privately owned business—regardless of how large or small—wasn't Adrian's main concern. She'd been raised in an orphanage and had learned discipline and self-worth at an early age. Her immediate problem upon deciding to enter the world of private enterprise had been the financing.

After almost an entire year of gathering data on her planned venture, plus an estimated cost of operation for the first year, Adrian presented her case to one of the vice-presidents of the bank where she kept her checking and savings accounts.

When, after carefully going over the information before him and after asking endless questions, the gentleman agreed to the loan, Adrian sat thunderstruck, unable to believe her good fortune.

The first six months were the roughest and she handled the office by herself. But hard work and a few good breaks enabled her to hire Sara Lindsey, a typist from the same firm where Adrian had been previously employed. Now for the twenty-six-year-old Adrian there was pride and an enormous sense of personal satisfaction as she rushed through each day and more often than not into the early evening as well.

She didn't look upon the long hours as an encroachment of her private life but as time spent toward helping her to become established as a successful businesswoman. She had a wonderful sense of humor and a flair for getting along with people, both traits being quite useful in achieving her ultimate goal.

A sharp buzz of the telephone jarred Adrian from her pleasant train of thought. She reached out and depressed the button, then lifted the receiver. "Yes, Sara?"

"Your number-one problem child is on the line, Adrian," the receptionist informed her in a harassed voice. "I tried to tell him that we didn't have anyone left to send over to him, but he insists on speaking with you."

"Thanks, Sara, but I've learned one thing about Simon Lord—he does like to have his own way." Adrian took a deep breath, tucked a strand of her deep auburn hair behind her ear, and then pushed another button on the phone panel. "This is Adrian

11

Kohl, Mr. Lord. What can I do for you?" Her voice was cool and brisk, her dark blue eyes flashing with annoyance.

"I believe that should be fairly obvious, Miss Kohl," the deep, raspy voice fairly growled over the line. "Upon the very flattering recommendation of Jason Lang, I decided to use the assistance of your agency in putting together a temporary office staff. And while the young woman you sent over to fill in as receptionist is very competent, your efforts so far to supply me with a secretary have been disastrous."

Adrian gripped the receiver in a surge of fury as the scathing words swept over her. Damn the man! She'd sent two of her best people to him, and they'd both left after only a day or two of enduring his horrible moods and irrational fits of temper.

"The two ladies I sent over, Mr. Lord, are both excellent secretaries. Don't you find it rather unusual that they both were unable to please you?" Adrian knew she was bordering on being impertinent, but the detestable man had done nothing but cause her trouble from the first moment she'd agreed to take him as a client.

"I'm not interested in your assessment of my personality, Miss Kohl," Simon Lord snapped. "You agreed to find me a secretary and I'm holding you to that agreement. Unless, that is, you feel you aren't capable of fulfilling the bargain," he tacked on in a not so subtle thrust at her level of competency.

With more self-control than she ever thought herself capable of, Adrian forced back the burning urge to tell this incredibly rude man precisely where he could go. But his unwitting remark—or had it been deliberate?—that she was somehow being given his business simply because Jason had "spoken" in her behalf, caused her to answer without really thinking.

"Don't worry, Mr. Lord. I'll have someone at your office by one o'clock. Will that be convenient?"

"Oh, yes, Miss Kohl, one o'clock will be fine. And, Miss Kohl, please make sure the lady is a mature adult. I've had about all I can stand of the teary-eyed goings-on of the southern-belle variety. Understand?"

"Perfectly. Good-bye, Mr. Lord." Adrian dropped the receiver with a decided thump. She leaned back in her chair, her fingers idly tapping the desk. At the moment it was difficult to decide who she was angrier with, Simon Lord or her fiancé, Jason Lang!

Jason had convinced her to do this small favor for him. "He's a powerful man, honey, and he's very influential," he'd urged Adrian.

"So you quite naturally thought to include me in the aura of generosity you're sure will come to both of us as a result of befriending Mr. Lord?" Adrian had asked, the faint amusement in her voice taking the sting out of her words.

"Well . . ." Jason hesitated, his grin somewhat sheepish. "I have to confess, I really wasn't that concerned about your business. Simon's thrown some of his legal work my way and I'm hoping for more."

"So what you're really saying is that you would like to keep on his good side."

"Of course." Jason sounded reproachful. "You know how difficult it is to get a law practice started. And while I'm doing quite well, any business from Simon Lord would be an added bonus."

Adrian had studied her fiancé across the width of the small, intimate table for two, the flickering light from the candle pointing out his boyish good looks. They'd been engaged for a year, and she still wouldn't set a definite date for the wedding.

Why? she asked herself in that brief moment of silent wondering. It was the same question she'd asked herself over and over. She'd always yearned for a family, ached to belong to someone. Jason offered her that security along with his love. So why wasn't she anxious to accept his gift and get on with their marriage?

"You're not annoyed with me, are you, sweetheart?" Jason cut into her thoughts. He reached across the table and caught her hand. "I mean," he shrugged, "my career is my main concern and, I hope, yours as well." He flashed that engaging grin that had always worked so beautifully in breaking down her defenses. "You know all the old clichés about the little woman behind the successful man. Well, that's what I want, honey."

But what about my wants? My needs? Adrian longed to ask, and then thought better of it. Jason had been raised by an overindulgent mother. There'd be time enough later on to point out that she too had a dream . . . ambitions, none of which she could visualize being submerged while she played the dutiful wife.

14

The conversation drifted on, with Adrian bringing up Simon Lord's name again by asking why he had arrived in Savannah without a private secretary.

"One of his aides said there'd been some mixup, some illness or something. I'm not quite sure. He's arranging for someone from his Denver branch to join him, but it will still be three weeks or so before she arrives."

"I see." Adrian accepted this bit of information with a sense of misgiving, then immediately wondered why. After all, she'd handled clients as important as this Lord person before. In most of her experiences, once she got past the bluff and bluster of their feeling of importance, she would find a likable human being.

"Are you sure, Adrian?" Sara exclaimed a while later, after having heard her friend's plan. "I know you go out on jobs when you have to, but this man. . . ." She shook her head. "He sounds like Attila the Hun."

"I know," Adrian said. "But he's also mean enough to spread the word that Kohl Temps can't live up to their contract."

"Well . . ." Sara hedged. "I suppose you do have a point. Just don't lose your cool. You've got a pretty good temper yourself." She grinned. "There's no doubt in my mind you'll ably defend our reputation. It's Mr. Lord I'm worried about. That poor man really has no idea what's in store for him."

"Ha!" Adrian grunted as she applied fresh lipstick. "He's the last person to need your pity."

* * *

At precisely ten minutes before one Adrian entered the building that housed a branch of one of the newest industries to come to Savannah. She quickly walked over and scanned the in-house directory, noting that Lord Enterprises occupied the entire second floor.

With determination in her graceful carriage and the set of her small chin, she entered the waiting elevator, pushed the second floor button, then leaned against the wall during the brief ride.

Her exit from the car was carried out with the same air of briskness. A short walk down a wide corridor brought her to the suite of offices she was seeking. Adrian grasped the knob and opened the door.

The scene before her might have appeared comical had it been anyone other than Simon Lord. There was, however, nothing humorous about the middle-aged man with the stump of a cigar clamped between his teeth. He had dispensed with his suit jacket, and the top two buttons of his white shirt were undone. His tie was somewhere between his chin and ear.

There was a menacing scowl on his weathered features as he barked into the receiver, telling the caller to wait. His other hand was reaching forward and jabbing the hold button as he answered yet another call. "Lord Enterprises!" he barked in a gravelly voice.

Closer inspection by Adrian revealed a complicated phone panel, lit up like a Christmas tree. As she walked toward the desk, the man who had been giving her such a difficult time for the past few days swiveled around in his chair and stared at the slim young woman.

"Hang on a minute, Pete." He then smiled. "What can I do for you, miss?" It was by far the warmest exchange to pass between Adrian and the heretofore faceless Simon Lord in days.

"I do believe, Mr. Lord, that that's my line." She grinned in spite of her ill will toward the man. "I'm Adrian Kohl. When we spoke this morning I promised to have someone here by one o'clock."

The man, acting totally out of character, or so she thought considering her past experience with him, simply continued to stare at Adrian, the tiniest flicker of amusement beginning to surface in his eyes.

"So you're Adrian Kohl." An engaging grin joined that mysterious twinkle. He extended a hand toward her across the width of the desk. "Not only am I pleased to meet you, Miss Kohl, I'm downright glad you're here."

Adrian had no choice but to accept his friendly gesture, meeting his outstretched hand with her slim one. "As you can see"—he nodded toward the glowing panel—"I'm not very good at this sort of thing. I'm sure—"

"Jake!" came a familiar thundering voice from somewhere in the direction of the office leading off the spacious reception room. "Where the hell is that damn file on Grannett?"

Adrian looked from the direction of the unfriendly voice to the pleasant countenance of the man sitting before her. "You're not Simon Lord." It was a statement rather than a question.

"No, ma'am. I'm Jake Tobias," he grinned. "I've been with Simon," he said, jerking his head toward the other office, "for a number of years. Now, if you'll excuse me, I'll go help him find that file and then I'll introduce you. By the way, would you mind taking over this contraption? I'm more at home out of doors than being tied to a desk."

"Of course, Mr. Tobias," Adrian agreed in a low voice. She walked around the desk and took the chair he'd vacated. "Is Mr. Lord aware of the calls that are waiting?"

He chuckled. "He sure is, honey. But hold 'em. Just take their number and Simon will get back to them. He's not used to being so available to anyone who calls. But, then, I'm not a receptionist." That fact Adrian could well attest to as she watched the loose-limbed gait of the gray-haired man as he entered Simon Lord's office.

"Well," she mused somewhat warily. "Mr. Lord seems to have old employees hopping to his beck and call as well as temporary ones."

She barely had time to stash her purse in an empty drawer and run a hand over the collar of the light blue dress she was wearing before the telephone began its insistent demands again.

Surely Carolyn Ames, the receptionist, should be back by now, Adrian thought wretchedly some twenty minutes later as she furiously scribbled down the name and number of a caller. She tore off the square piece of paper and added it to the growing

18

stack of messages, then raised one hand to her nape and gently massaged the tense muscles of her neck.

There was a slow burn beginning to consume Adrian. Even though he'd been tied up on the telephone since her arrival, the all-powerful Mr. Lord could have at least taken the time to quickly introduce himself. Perhaps he thought by ignoring her it would serve to place her at a disadvantage. Had he only known, feeling at a disadvantage was the furthest thing from Adrian's mind. She was becoming angrier by the second.

She had just finished taking down another message and was about to add it to the others when the door to the adjoining office was flung open. Adrian looked up from where she was seated, her blue eyes—the color heightened by her emotional state—meeting the openly appraising brown ones of a tall, deeply tanned man.

In that first brief moment during the collision of their gazes, Adrian felt as though her body had received an electrical shock. She found herself unashamedly returning the searing look, as well as studying the rough, almost harshly carved features of the man's face.

There was nothing of the conventional handsomeness about him, she noted, the cruel harshness lending a toughness that was oddly appealing. Appealing, but in no way detracting from the innate maleness of the man.

Luxurious dark hair barely brushed a broad forehead. Thick brows grew above the most compelling pair of brown eyes she'd ever seen. The nose was almost hawkish in its prominence, his lips full and sensual.

There were other qualities in his face that stood out, not the least of which was his strong jaw and determined chin. Further inspection revealed broad shoulders and a thick chest tapering into a narrow waist that led Adrian to wonder how a man as busy as he obviously was kept in shape.

"Miss Kohl? I'm Simon Lord." His tone of voice was indicative of a pleasant individual, completely at variance with the madman who'd been making her miserable for the last few days. "I'm sorry, but I was delayed by the telephone."

"Mr. Lord." Adrian nodded as she watched him move across the room and stop on the other side of the desk. His entire being exuded such an aura of intimidation, such a threatening air, that for one fraction of a second Adrian was tempted to grab her purse and run.

He stood waiting, minus his tie, the sleeves of his white shirt rolled back to reveal strong tanned forearms covered by a scattering of silky black hairs. "Have you come to look over the place? See if I'm really as bad as your girls reported me to be?" he asked mockingly.

"Not at all, Mr. Lord. Didn't Mr. Tobias tell you? I was unable to get in touch with the only other person I had left to send to you, so . . ." She shrugged one shoulder in a confident manner and smiled. "I came to fill in for this afternoon. However," she added, thinking she might as well clear up one glaring oversight immediately, "if your secretary has to double as receptionist, then I can certainly understand part of the problem." She regarded him levelly, determined to stand her ground.

"Believe me, Miss Kohl, answering the telephone was not one of the duties of your ladies. Though considering the sizable fee I'll be paying you, I don't think it's too much to ask that they be competent in typing and shorthand."

"They are competent, Mr. Lord, but even with the most efficient of secretaries, there can be a clash of personalities," she smoothly countered.

"So you've decided to see for yourself if I'm an overbearing brute? Rushing into the fray to protect your unblemished reputation." He made her sound like a frustrated hen hovering over her two chicks.

"That's not the reason at all. But if you remember, I did promise to have someone over here at one."

"Do you often do this sort of thing?" he asked curiously, his eyes never still as they wandered over her shoulder-length hair, the slightly upward thrust of her eyebrows at the outer edges, her deep blue eyes, and, lastly, the inviting fullness of her lips.

"Fill in on an assignment when there's no one else available?" Adrian asked, finding the boldness of his gaze disconcerting. She could feel the warmth as his eyes did a quick, curious survey of her body.

"Yes. What happens if the customer requests a mechanic or a cook?" he grinned rakishly.

"Why, then . . . I'd simply refer them to someone else," she replied. "But in case you need a mechanic or a cook, I just happen to have one of each available

21

at the moment." Her gaze never wavered as she braved his attempt to place her at a disadvantage.

In a gesture that was deliberate, Adrian lifted her left arm and looked at her watch. "Don't you think we should get started? I'd hate to think you aren't getting your money's worth."

"As you wish, Miss Kohl," Simon murmured silkily, one hand gesturing her toward the office beyond. His eyes were riveted to the gleam of the engagement ring on her left hand. "Have you set the date for your wedding?" The question caught her completely off-guard.

Unconsciously the fingers of Adrian's hands clenched into two small fists. "No, we haven't set a date." She wondered what on earth had prompted the question . . . plus her own disquiet at the probing.

"Aren't you worried that some other woman will steal your fiancé away from you?" he asked on a derisive note. "Aren't you frustrated because you can't legally bind your man to your side before fate intervenes and wrests him from you?"

Adrian stared incredulously at this horribly rude person. "Frankly, Mr. Lord, I don't think either of your questions deserves an answer. But just to set the record straight, I'm the one who hasn't seen fit to set a date, not my fiancé." Her patience was at an end with this man, and she resented his questions.

"Now," Adrian said, impatiently tapping one foot. "If you still need someone to help you, I suggest we get on with it. If not, I have other things to do."

Not once did she allow her gaze to waver as she

spoke. Job or no job, she refused to be intimidated or quizzed about her personal life by anyone.

"Touché, Miss Kohl." Simon Lord inclined his head mockingly. "By all means, let's get on with the job at hand." He moved then, far quicker than Adrian had expected. Almost before she was aware of it, he was beside her, his large hand grasping her elbow.

His forward progress through an attractive office, obviously waiting for his personal secretary, and then into his own domain was just as forceful as was everything else she'd observed about the man. Average in height, and having to match his much longer strides, Adrian walked at a faster pace than normal in order for it not to appear that she was being dragged.

Once inside the spacious room that bore the definite stamp of total masculinity in its furnishings, their headlong rush was halted. Simon Lord released his grip on her elbow and waved her to a chair.

He strode around the massive desk and sat down. The enormous amount of clutter on his desk clearly attested to the fact that indeed he did need a secretary.

During the time it took him to sort through one particular stack of correspondence that seemed to hold his attention more than any of the others, Adrian looked around the office.

There was a nicely balanced blend of soft wheaten and rust tones in the carpet and draperies. Indirect lighting combined with the large sweeping windows to give an excellent view of the city. An extra-long sofa and two comfortable chairs in gleaming brown leather provided a cozy arrangement at one end of the room. Somehow Adrian found it difficult to imagine her client making use of that convenient placement of furniture, picturing him instead at the head of a long, polished table, browbeating his board members into submission.

"Daydreaming, Miss Kohl?" the raspy, gravelly voice she'd come to hate cut into her thoughts.

Adrian made a point of calmly transferring her direct gaze from its casual perusal of the room to the man who was glaring at her across the desk.

"Not at all, Mr. Lord. I was simply giving you time to look through your correspondence." She held up pencil and pad. "I'm ready when you are."

For what seemed like an incredible length of time but couldn't have been more than a few seconds, dark eyes waged a silent war with deep blue ones. During that visual exchange Adrian felt a curious shiver creep over her body. It was comparable to the reaction one experiences when narrowly escaping an accident. It was unnerving, and one she disliked.

It became evident to Adrian as she took letter after letter that regardless of how annoying the man was, Simon Lord hadn't been exaggerating one bit when he'd said he was up to his neck with work.

The nature of his corporation was diversified and complicated, causing a grudging admiration to emerge as she listened to him and absorbed the rapier-sharp decisions he made.

Later, as she typed, Adrian couldn't help but hope his own staff arrived soon. Keeping him supplied with office personnel, even temporarily, could prove to be her undoing. And she certainly had no intention of taking him on herself, she grimly reflected as she removed the final page of the last letter from the typewriter.

With arms and shoulders that felt laden down with huge weights, Adrian rose to her feet and stretched. She scooped up the stack of letters and walked to the door of Simon Lord's private office and knocked.

At his curt order to come in she mentally braced herself for the full brunt of his unsettling gaze and opened the door.

"These are ready for your signature, Mr. Lord," she announced as she walked over to his desk and placed the neatly finished letters in front of him. Rather than stand in his presence like some child waiting to be punished, Adrian sat down in the chair she'd previously occupied and prepared to wait for him to check over the letters.

Not that there would be any errors, she thought to herself, but since they were unfamiliar with each other's work habits, she thought it proper on her part to wait for any changes he might care to make.

Simon chose to ignore her for several minutes, then thrust aside the file he'd been studying and glanced at his watch. "Too much for you, Miss Kohl?" he asked in a grouchy voice.

"I beg your pardon?" she asked, somewhat baffled by his question.

"The number of letters I gave you," he said impatiently. "Have you decided to come back in the morning and finish them?"

"If you'll check, you'll see that I've typed all the

letters you gave me, Mr. Lord," she replied. "I'm waiting to see if you wish to make any corrections or additions before they're mailed."

For a moment Adrian was tempted to laugh at the dark scowl that swept over the craggy features of his face. Obviously Simon Lord wasn't used to anyone, especially a woman, daring to disagree with his thoughts or opinions.

A grim silence settled over the room as he lifted the first letter and briefly scanned its contents. During this time Adrian found herself unable to pull her eyes away from him. It was as though some deep, mysterious compulsion had her in its grip, causing her to want to know more about the huge man sitting opposite her.

With inexplicable fascination, she watched the way he ran the back of his free hand beneath his chin as he concentrated. She noted the way the edges of his sideburns seemed to turn inward, gently cupping the tan skin at the side of his face. His hair was cut reasonably short, the neckline barely brushing the collar of his shirt.

There was a tiny scar at the edge of one dark brow, adding a slightly satanic look to his expression. Adrian envied him the thick, dark lashes that fringed his piercing eyes. Her gaze was finally drawn to his hands, which were large, in perfect harmony with the rest of his body, the nails clipped short. She also knew there was strength in those hands. She'd felt it when he'd grasped her elbow.

As if sensing the close scrutiny he was being subjected to, Simon raised his eyes and met Adrian's openly appraising stare. Her first impulse was to look away, but she found herself unable to do so. It was the same as the first moment their eyes had met—the initial impact, some inexplicable force transmitting an even more indecipherable message between them.

With superhuman effort Adrian did break the force of their gazes, furious with herself as she felt her cheeks reddening. Thankfully, the source responsible for her discomfort refrained from commenting, and returned to his study of the letters before him.

"I must compliment you, Miss Kohl. Every I is dotted and every T is crossed. Everything is beautifully done." The maddening man finally spoke precisely at the exact moment Adrian thought she would scream with frustration.

She was anxious to get away from Simon Lord. His presence was disturbing, and Adrian knew it went far deeper than a mere disagreement with him over her efforts to find him a secretary. In a nutshell . . . he was dangerous!

"Thank you," Adrian answered quietly. She rose to her feet. "Shall I see that they're mailed?"

"Oh, Miss Ames will be more than happy to handle that for you out of sheer gratitude that she wasn't called on to type them in the first place." His tone was one of dry amusement. "Tell me, Miss Kohl," Simon drawled, rising to his feet and coming around the desk. He leaned comfortably against the edge of the massive fixture, his hands braced against the surface on either side of him. "Would you be interested in accepting the position as my private secretary?"

For one wild moment Adrian could do nothing

more than stare at him, then she hastily shook her head. "I already have a job, Mr. Lord," she reminded him, adding a few more feet to the space between them by backing toward the door. "I'm quite happy. I'm sure that once your own secretary joins you, things will be back to normal."

"How can you be *sure,* Miss Kohl?" he asked with a bite.

"Why . . . it's . . . Why shouldn't it?" Adrian stammered, itching to be on her way, gone from the unsettling force that surrounded this man.

"Mrs. Donet won't be joining me. She recently found out that she's pregnant. I'd hoped to find someone here in Savannah," he explained.

"Which I'm sure you will do. But you must understand that my agency offers only temporary help. I rarely get applicants who are interested in permanent employment. Any of the other agencies would be better suited to handle your particular needs."

"Just what would you know about my 'particular' needs, Miss Kohl?" The ambiguity of the question brought a heated warmth to her face.

"Your need for a secretary, Mr. Lord, nothing more. Anything else you require will have to be taken care of by someone else."

For several seconds Adrian withstood the angry gaze that raked her slender frame. *God!* she thought as she forcibly controlled her breathing. *This man is as lethal as a time bomb!*

"Why do I get the feeling that you dislike me, Miss Kohl?" Simon broke the stormy silence that was heady in its own reckless fashion.

"But I hardly know you, Mr. Lord," Adrian said softly. "I have no feelings one way or the other."

"Are you in love with Jason Long?" he asked bluntly.

"Don't you think that's a rather ridiculous question?"

"Will you have dinner with me?" He again caught her off-guard by abruptly switching topics of conversation.

"No," Adrian softly answered. Inwardly she was shocked and somewhat embarrassed to find herself wondering what it would be like to sit across from him with candlelight flickering against his dark features, and, later, to feel his lips against hers.

"Why not?" Simon asked mockingly, a lazy smile touching his attractive lips. "Are you afraid your boyfriend will object? He won't, believe me."

"That's not a very nice insinuation," she replied in a crisp voice. "And for your information, I'm the one who doesn't want to have dinner with you. My refusal certainly doesn't stem from any fear of Jason's disapproval." She turned and walked toward the door, then stopped and looked over her shoulder at Simon. "On second thought, Mr. Lord, I'm afraid my agency can no longer take care of you. Your *needs* will have to be seen to by someone who thinks along the same lines that you do."

She walked through the doorway, grasped the knob, and quietly closed the door behind her. It wasn't until she'd retrieved her purse and was in the corridor waiting for the elevator that she realized she was holding her breath!

CHAPTER TWO

Fortunately for Adrian, she was one of those red-heads who wasn't troubled with an overabundance of freckles. Only in the hottest part of summer, if she stayed in the sun for too long, would she get the faintest sprinkling across her nose. Not that she cared in the least.

She was pretty in the peaches 'n' cream fashion, but could be better described as striking. Her eyes were her strongest feature, and skillful use of makeup enhanced their beauty.

It was this careful task she was engaged in when she heard the sound of the doorbell.

"Darn!" she muttered, quickly smoothing the last of the medium blue shadow over her lids. She stared critically at her reflection, then grabbed a tissue from the box sitting on the dressing table and wiped her hands.

A repeated sound of the bell sent her scurrying from the bedroom. When she at last flung open the door, Jason was leaning against the doorjamb, a grin on his face.

"It's about time," he said good-naturedly as he pushed himself upright, eyeing the terry-cloth robe that hit his fiancée mid-thigh. "Hmmm . . . why don't we skip Mother's cocktail party altogether?"

"I'm sorry, Jason," Adrian said in an attempt to distract his train of thought. She quickly stepped back for him to enter the room. "I was held up and didn't get home until about thirty minutes ago." She brushed her lips against his cheek and deftly stepped from the circle of his arms. She wasn't in the mood for a passionate embrace.

Jason was a tall, handsome man with blond hair and blue eyes. They'd met at a party over a year ago, and he'd immediately been captivated by the laughing redhead with the flashing eyes and the bubbly personality. Their love wasn't the exciting, breathless experience Adrian had often dreamed of, but it was steady and enduring, and that meant more to her than a brief flash of passion. Jason filled the void that loneliness and fear had created.

"What held you up this time? Were you sitting with some old maid's parrot?" Jason asked, making no effort to hide his amusement at the variety of requests that came in to her office.

"No," Adrian said over her shoulder on her way to the small kitchen. "I was detained by your friend, Simon Lord." She took down a glass from one of the cupboards, dropped in two ice cubes, added a jigger of Scotch, a dash of Perrier water, then stirred the mixture and handed it to Jason.

"If it was Simon Lord who was responsible for your tardiness, then don't apologize," Jason offered expansively.

Adrian screwed the cap back on the Scotch and returned it to the cupboard before turning to face him. "Why on earth should it matter whether Simon Lord or Joe Blow held me up? Why should he receive preferential treatment?"

"Come on, Adrian. Surely you aren't so naive as to discount the man's importance. Not only has he bought out a company that was slowly sinking, he's adding to it and making Savannah a branch of his vast holdings."

"All of which is nice, I'm sure. But what has that got to do with me?" she asked in that mulish way she had when she wanted to be especially difficult. She knew exactly what Jason was getting at and it angered her.

"We've already been through this, honey. I thought I explained it to you the other evening at dinner. Simon makes it a habit to employ local people when he moves into a new area. That's one of the reasons for his overwhelming success. He's shrewd enough to see that local support is important when any large corporation settles in a new town."

"And all his shrewd business sense is supposed to make me happy that he has the manners of a boor? That he caused me to have to work late?" The sharpness in her voice bounced off the walls like a ricocheting bullet.

"Of course not," Jason muttered in an uncomfortable manner. "But it could mean an added retainer for my law practice if he sees how eager we are to make his transition here a little easier."

For one wild moment Adrian was tempted to slap Jason's face. How was it possible for one man to be so anxious to please another person that he would become a smiling, subservient fool? But she knew the answer even before she asked it.

His mother. Stella Lang, trying desperately to maintain a toehold on the fringes of a society in which she thought she should be rightfully included, had for years filled her son's mind with just such outlandish nonsense as he'd just spouted regarding Simon Lord.

At one time the Lang name had held a place of prominence in Savannah. Unfortunately the grasping Stella latched on to Jason's father in the waning years of that prominence. Her husband's death had left her with a pleasant town house, money from his insurance, and a burning desire to reestablish herself in that social set. However, her forced gentility overshadowed whatever nicer qualities she might have had, if any, leaving a brittle, aggressive woman who used every bit of conniving at her disposal to attain her goals. Jason was proving to be a useful extension of her ambitions.

"Well, I'm afraid you'll have to look to other means of support in securing Mr. Lord's legal business, Jason. I informed him in no uncertain terms that I no longer cared to have him as a client," Adrian told her startled fiancé. "Enjoy your drink.

I'll only be a few more minutes," she threw over her shoulder as she swept from the room.

Adrian hated the command performances she and Jason were subjected to by his mother, and this particular evening was proving to be more disastrous than usual.

Approximately once a month Stella would host a cocktail party. Always in attendance were one or more young women whom she considered more suitable for her son than Adrian.

On this occasion Cheryl Adams was the bait. She was a quiet, shy girl, who would probably be the perfect wife for Jason, Adrian grudgingly thought some hour and a half later as she made her way toward the laughing couple.

After exchanging pleasantries and briefly chatting, Adrian drew Jason aside.

"Don't you think we should be leaving? Sandra's party starts at eight, and I did promise to help her."

"Is it time?" Jason asked. He pushed back his cuff and glanced at his watch. "Sorry, honey. I didn't realize it was so late. Let's say good-bye to Mother and be on our way."

"Er . . . why don't you go ahead. I'll just wait here for you," Adrian suggested.

Already Stella had raised Adrian's hackles by suggesting that when Adrian started to choose her trousseau she hoped she'd be allowed to help.

"How sweet of you to offer, Stella," Adrian had replied between gritted teeth, knowing nothing on

34

earth could induce her to go shopping with the woman.

"Good dress sense is a must, my dear. When you marry Jason, you'll be carrying the Lang name, and your appearance will be very important," Stella said in sugary tones, coating the knife-edged sharpness of her true feelings.

The two women stared at each other, both wearing smiles that to the casual observer appeared genuine. Only they knew the depths of their dislike for each other.

"Believe me, Stella, I'll do my best not to embarrass you. By the way, was your husband's mother as generous to you when you married Jason's father?" Adrian innocently asked. "I hope so, for I'm sure it must have been most difficult for you, not coming from the same social background as the Langs."

"Why, you—" the older woman started, her rage enhanced by the twin spots of color that turned her cheeks a garish red.

"Please excuse me, Stella. I see Jason and Cheryl." At that point Adrian had whisked herself away from the murderous gleam in her hostess's eye without a backward glance.

During the ride to Sandra's house Adrian was quieter than usual. She couldn't put her finger on the reason for her silent state, merely aware that she felt adrift, restless.

There were a number of cars parked in the driveway of the sprawling, cedar-shingled house that belonged to Sandra and David Cromier, causing Jason to mutter darkly as he looked for a place to park.

"I thought this was supposed to be a small party," he said as he maneuvered the car into the last available spot.

"So did I," Adrian agreed. "Apparently David added to the guest list without consulting Sandra."

Before Adrian could open the door and get out of the car, Jason laid a detaining hand on her arm. "What's wrong, honey?" he softly asked. "Ever since we left Mother's you've hardly said a word. Did the two of you clash again?"

"Of course not," she laughed huskily. "Your mother and I understand each other perfectly, Jason. Why, she even offered to help me choose my trousseau. What makes you think we quarreled?"

"Oh, just something she . . ." He shook his head and sighed. "It was nothing. I just hope you can learn to get along with Mother. She's really not well, Adrian, and she's very dear to me. As a matter of fact, she suggested something the other day that seems the perfect solution for us."

"Oh?" Adrian slowly asked. "What was her suggestion?"

"Since the town house is so handy to both our offices, Mother thinks it would be an excellent idea for us to live with her after we're married."

"What did you tell her, Jason?"

"That I'd talk it over with you, of course. But frankly, honey, I'm all for it. Just think, we'd have our own built-in baby-sitter. Plus I'd be able to keep a careful eye on Mother," he smiled, enormously pleased with himself.

"I really don't think we need to be concerned with

baby-sitters at the moment, Jason. As for living with your mother . . ." Adrian shook her head. "I don't want us to live with anyone. I want us to have our own home."

"Couldn't you at least give it a try, Adrian?" he gently prodded. "I know you have a certain resentment toward Mother, but if you'd only give her a chance, I'm sure you would come to love her as much as I do."

In a pig's eye! Adrian was tempted to shout. Resentment was certainly the key word, but Jason was confused. Stella was the one eaten up with resentment. She had to keep her son close to her, and she knew Adrian would never allow such a thing once they were married. *How can I make him see his mother for what she really is?* Adrian thought. *Worse still, do I really want to become involved in the effort?*

"Regardless of whatever relationship your mother and I have, Jason, I still refuse to move in with her," she told him as gently as she could. There was no point in making him think she would even consider the suggestion.

"You sound decidedly ominous, honey." Jason tried for a teasing note. "Are you beginning to have second thoughts about becoming Mrs. Jason Lang?"

Adrian stared at the smiling face before her, at the boyish grin that curved his lips. His features were soft and round, nothing at all like the chiseled granite of Simon Lord's face. That individual would have no trouble at all in coping with a clinging mother. But Jason? He would always find it difficult refusing Stella Lang.

"Doesn't every girl wonder a thousand times before the wedding if she's doing the right thing?" she smiled brightly. "After all, we women are supposed to be fickle, aren't we?"

The sounds of the party could be heard as Adrian and Jason neared the double carport and the back door. That entrance was used by family and close friends, and Adrian barely slowed down as she knocked on the door, then burst into the kitchen.

"Well," Sandra cried. "It's about time. I was beginning to think you'd forgotten." She hurried over and kissed both newcomers on their cheeks. "Jason, the bar is set up on the patio. It's a bit nippy, but David insisted on inviting an army. I'm going to steal your girl for a while, okay?" the pert and very pregnant blonde ran on.

"Just so long as I can get an occasional glance at her," Jason grinned. He squeezed Adrian's hand. "See you later, honey." He kissed her on the cheek and left the room.

"So," Adrian began as soon as they were alone. "Why did you allow David to turn your party into a mob scene, and what do I need to do first?"

"This," Sandra said as she indicated an assortment of cheeses and crackers to be arranged on a large tray. "As for the increased number of guests, I simply gave in as I usually do when we entertain."

"As simple as that, eh?" Adrian grinned.

"Of course," the other answered. "But each little defeat has its moments of reward. Remember that when you and Jason marry. By the way, you're a knockout in that dress. Stay away from David. You

38

might prove to be more of a temptation than he can resist."

"Heavens, Sandra!" Adrian exclaimed as she set about helping her friend. "You get worse as you get older. Trying to keep track of your ramblings is comparable to being lost in a maze," she laughingly kidded her friend.

Sandra merely smiled at the gentle ribbing. "Being vague has its uses. By the way, how were you able to keep your intended from attacking you in that creation?" She stared longingly at the blue dress and the way it clung to Adrian's figure.

"Easily," Adrian replied in a stony voice. "We were discussing his mother."

"Ah." Sandra nodded knowingly. "I can see how that subject could cool the most fervent ardor. Is she still causing trouble?"

"You could say that. Her latest efforts surpass all previous ones. She thinks we should move in with her once we're married."

Sandra was quiet for a moment as she thought over this latest effort on Stella's behalf to break up her son's engagement. "You did object, didn't you?"

"Need you ask?" Adrian retorted darkly. "I felt much like a stern parent denying her child a special treat." She shook her head. "I don't know, Sandra. I'm beginning to view marriage with Jason in the same vein as going to the dentist—the only sensible thing to do, but quite uncomfortable in the process."

"I think all us gals have doubts, honey," Sandra consoled her friend. Privately, she wasn't so sure. While he was a warm and loving person, Jason Lang simply wasn't the right man for Adrian. Their personalities were reversed, with Adrian being the stronger, the more dominating of the two.

"By the way, there's someone here this evening that I want you to meet. He's a friend of David's and he's new in town. He's also disgustingly wealthy and single." Sandra placed one forefinger against her chin and considered her friend for several seconds. "Perhaps an exciting fling with a handsome rake is what's needed in your life before you settle down to domestic bliss."

Adrian turned and stared at her friend, her mouth slightly agape. "Has your pregnancy affected your mind, you goose? I hardly think an affair would solve anything. Honestly, Sandra, you're totally bonkers."

"Oh, well." Sandra lifted one shoulder indifferently. "I suppose you know best. But if I were single, I'd find it very difficult to resist Simon Lord."

"Simon Lord? *The* Simon Lord that bought out Terrel Electronics?" Adrian asked incredulously.

"Of course. Do you know him?" Sandra said over her shoulder as she spooned avocado dip into two bowls.

"I certainly do," Adrian snapped as she placed the last of the crackers on the serving dish. She picked up a towel and wiped her hands. "I let Jason talk me into taking him on as a client, and I've regretted it ever since. He's rude and overbearing, and I really don't care for him."

"Er . . . aren't you being a wee bit hard on the man?" Sandra asked in a peculiarly strained voice.

"No way, sweetie. So, if it's Simon Lord you've

chosen as my lover in the affair you think will cure my considerable ills, then forget it. I'm not interested."

"Now, that's a challenge no man worth his salt can ignore, Miss Kohl," came a deep, vibrant voice from directly behind Adrian.

She whirled about and found herself mere inches from the same man she'd just been berating. There was amusement and daring lurking in the mysterious depths of his laughing eyes as he returned her embarrassed gaze.

Adrian looked beyond the intimidating solidness of Simon Lord to Sandra, who was leaning against the counter, her hands braced against the surface on either side of her. There was such a bemused expression on her face, Adrian wanted to shake her.

"I—I did try to warn you," Sandra stammered.

Simon turned, including his hostess in the warm smile that softened the hard features of his face. "Don't let what Miss Kohl said bother you, Sandra. I've heard worse. In fact, I find it refreshing to meet a woman who speaks her mind."

"Oh?" Sandra spoke somewhat dryly. "Then you're in for a most enjoyable evening. Adrian has never been known for her tact. Now, if you two will excuse me, I'll take this dip out to the patio. Enjoy yourselves."

"Don't bother, Sandra. I'll take—" Adrian started forward, only to see her friend's back disappear with a swish through the swinging door.

"Afraid, Miss Kohl?" Simon asked in an infuriatingly amused voice.

41

Adrian turned and faced him—the heightened glow in her cheeks proclaiming louder than words her state of agitation. For a moment she simply stared at him. And yet there was no need to go over his face feature by feature. She remembered each minute detail from their last meeting. Certainly nothing had changed, unless it was the reaffirming impact upon her senses of his total masculinity.

"No, Mr. Lord, I'm not afraid." She shrugged. "I think embarrassed is a better word." She smiled in spite of herself. "It's rather like having someone walk into a room and catch you talking to yourself. Hasn't that ever happened to you?" Adrian asked as she began removing Swedish meatballs from a pan and arranging them in a chafing dish. "Would you mind adding the toothpicks?" she asked unconcernedly.

"Not at all," Simon replied, quickly masking the smile that threatened to break through at this cavalier treatment. "Isn't your friend Sandra taking on more than she should by having so many people in?"

"Of course. That's why her mother-in-law or I find ourselves forced into service when there's a party. Even as a child Sandra was impetuous."

"You've known each other for a number of years?" he asked, finding it very entertaining to be poking toothpicks into Swedish meatballs and at the same time carrying on a conversation with this beautiful woman.

"Yes. We were both raised in an orphanage. We're like sisters, only closer I think."

"And very independent, mmm?"

Adrian chuckled. "Does it show that much?" She

42

looked up at Simon then, and almost caught her breath at the force that traveled between them. With considerable effort on her part, she forced her attention back to the job at hand.

"I'm afraid so," he scowled. "Twice in one day I've been subjected to that wicked tongue of yours. You've really pricked my ego."

"Then please accept the humble apologies of a poor working woman—for her unkind words, that is. I refuse to accept responsibility for the state of your ego."

"Independent, sassy, and beautiful. That's an interesting combination, Miss Kohl," he said with narrowed eyes.

"Thank you, sir. We southern belles do aim to please."

"Ouch! I see you remember that little mistake."

"Vividly. Don't you know better than to cast aspersions on the very backbone of the South by making snide remarks regarding its women?"

"Er . . . I think I'm beginning to," Simon grinned. "By the way, can't we drop the formality? Addressing each other as Miss Kohl or Mr. Lord seems rather silly in view of the circumstances. Agreed?"

It was several seconds before Adrian could bring herself to look up at him. When she did, it was as though she were agreeing to a lot more than their being on a first-name basis.

CHAPTER THREE

Early on the morning after Sandra's party Adrian sat at her desk, one hand idly twirling a pencil, the other holding the receiver to her ear. There was an expression of patient resignation on her face as she listened to the voice on the other end of the line.

"Throckmorton isn't really a dog, you understand, Miss Kohl. He believes he's a person. So naturally I would insist that the individual you choose to care for him be extremely sensitive to someone as intelligent as he is."

"Of course, Mrs. Neville," Adrian murmured reassuringly, her softly worded response barely interrupting the lengthy monologue of the anxious woman.

"I would also insist on meeting the young woman, Miss Kohl. Throckmorton doesn't care for men. You do remember, don't you?"

"Certainly, Mrs. Neville. I still have the complete workup on Throckmorton that you gave me the first time you used our agency," Adrian replied. "Miss Jagger, who is a graduate student, will be looking after your baby. She's done this sort of thing before for us, and has excellent references in case you would like to check her out."

"Oh, I'm sure that won't be necessary," Mrs. Neville twittered. "I have complete trust in your decision."

"Thank you," Adrian smiled. "I'll have Miss Jagger come over to your apartment later this afternoon. The two of you can meet . . . get acquainted. You can also give her the key."

Even with her expertise in handling trying clients, another five minutes elapsed before Adrian cradled the receiver and then rubbed her throbbing ear.

The door of her office opened and Sara entered, a knowing grin on her face. "Am I correct in assuming that we are being honored again by looking after Throckmorton?" she asked as she placed a stack of mail on the desk.

"Yes, and for four long weeks." Adrian sighed. She ran a smoothing hand over her fall of dark auburn hair, her pansy-blue eyes revealing the lack of sleep from the night before. "I wish we were in a position to turn down Mrs. Neville's business. But," she shrugged, "seeing after her spoiled sheepdog will add a nice boost to this month's receipts."

Sara sat down in the chair at one end of Adrian's desk, and together they began opening and sorting the mail.

45

"Mmm . . ." the perky blond receptionist murmured as she held up a check. "Colonel Redford has been extremely prompt in paying, hasn't he?" She eyed the amount as she passed the check to Adrian.

"Indeed he has, and I hope he continues to pursue his hobby for many years to come."

Sara smiled. "Exactly how long has he been researching the novel he intends writing?"

"At least six years." Adrian smiled back at her. "Between you and me, I think he simply enjoys traveling about and meeting people."

"Well, whatever the reasons, he seems to be a perfect doll to work for. We never have any complaints from the girls who type his notes for him."

Adrian agreed. Unfortunately, all her clients weren't so easily pleased. Her first order of business for the day had been to make sure Lillian Sorres was at Simon's office. It was after ten, and so far there hadn't been a hysterical outburst from Mrs. Sorres, nor a fit of temper from Simon.

Simon Lord. He was by far the most intriguing man Adrian had ever met, and one she was unable to get out of her mind.

Their encounter the night before in Sandra's kitchen hadn't been the only exchange between them during the evening. It seemed that every time Adrian turned around, Simon was at her elbow, talking . . . smiling. And if he wasn't there, her eyes weren't content until they sought him out in the crowd, lingering on the dark head, the width of his shoulders, and finally meeting and holding his gaze in an exchange of awareness—the balance so fragile, so delicate, she was afraid of it being crushed.

After one particularly hectic period of helping a worn-out Sandra whip up some extra food, Adrian found herself wanting to be alone. The party was nice and the guests friendly, but she felt uneasy. It was as though she were waiting for something to happen and hadn't the faintest idea what that something was.

She wandered into the empty living room, finally coming to a halt in one darkened corner. The sounds of voices raised in laughter and conversation melted into a pleasant hum as Adrian leaned her forehead against the cool glass of the window, her eyes staring unseeing into the night.

Ironically enough, it wasn't her problems with Jason that crowded the corridors of her mind, but the image of Simon Lord. Adrian closed her eyes and sighed, wondering at this sudden intense interest in a man she'd only known for a few hours. But she was interested, even though she recognized the futility of such fanciful flights of the imagination.

She was engaged to Jason. He was a kind, considerate man. *So why don't I set a date for our wedding?* she asked herself, and then inhaled deeply as her eyes became glazed with the unshed brilliance of tears. She hadn't even given thought to any of the usual details most women begin worrying about the minute they become engaged. Was she some sort of misfit, who enjoyed stringing a man along? Had her childhood left her wanting to be loved but unable to accept love from a man?

"Adrian?"

Without turning she recognized the voice. She opened her eyes and saw his reflection behind her. Tall, bronze, and wide—the epitome of unleashed strength. Yet she'd seen a gentleness in him during the evening and a sense of humor.

"What brings you in here, Simon?" she asked in a hushed voice as she continued to stare at their reflections.

"I was looking for you." No pretense, no attempt at hiding what he wanted. Without him seeming to move, Adrian felt his hands on her shoulders, turning her around to face him. With the same fluid ease one huge hand brushed upward over her body and cupped her nape, his touch warming her skin. "I couldn't find you at first and I panicked," he murmured huskily.

"Simon—" she began, only to have him place a finger against her lips.

"Hush," he quietly commanded her. "I don't want to hear it. Right now you're unhappy and I'm here. Pretend we're the only two people in the world."

"But Jason—"

"Forget Jason. He doesn't exist," he whispered as he bent his head and drew her to him all in the same move. His lips seemed to hover momentarily over hers. In that brief space of time Adrian meant to pull back. Some instinct warned her that not to do so would be disastrous. But Simon was quicker. Lips that had hesitated now began a dizzying seduction that blanked all thoughts from her mind but that of responding.

The taste of him caught at her as she opened her mouth to him, the smell of him and the tangy after-shave he wore becoming a part of her. His mouth that she'd thought in their first meeting to be sensuous and cruel was both those things, but infinitely gentle as well. His tongue plundered hers, but wasn't overbearing; demanded, but gave as well.

And Adrian gave . . . and gave, until she thought she would cry out from wanting him. When his mouth withdrew from hers and sought the wildly throbbing pulse beneath her ear, it seemed the most natural thing in the world for her to ease her head back so that his lips would meet no restriction.

Even when she felt the warmth of a hand cup and hold her breast, Adrian offered no resistance. It was as though time were indeed standing still, and she and Simon really were the only two people in the world.

Then with a slow and painful realization Adrian felt him withdrawing, felt the total oneness of only seconds ago slipping away. Once more the noise of the party emerged from the background, reminding her of another commitment, a commitment to another man.

Simon, sensing her distress, retained his hold on her nape. He also grasped her chin as well. "Now I know why no date has been set for the wedding. But what puzzles me even more is why you're pretending to love Jason Lang," he rasped in a voice made husky from passion.

"But I do love him." Adrian closed her eyes against the dark, knowing gaze. He was looking into her very soul and she couldn't allow him that privilege. "Please, Simon, leave it." There was pain in her eyes and a vulnerability, now that he knew a part of what she was feeling.

"Will you have lunch with me tomorrow?"

"No, Simon."

"Oh, yes, Adrian," he softly mimicked. "How you handle it is your business, but you will have lunch with me." He leaned down and brushed his lips against hers before she could stop him. "Until tomorrow, Adrian," he murmured, and then turned and left.

"Well, that takes care of the mail," Sara said in an amused voice as she rose to her feet and threw a grin toward her startled employer.

Adrian glanced first at the stack of opened correspondence and then at Sara, a look of chagrin on her face. "I'm sorry. My mind was somewhere else."

"I could tell," Sara laughed. "By the way, what time will you be going to lunch?"

"I'm flexible. Do you have something you need to do?"

"Actually, I'm meeting Mark and his mother. I was hoping to take an extra half hour if it's okay with you."

"Take all the time you need," Adrian told her. "I was planning on calling Smitty's and having a sandwich sent over anyway." And that, she congratulated herself, will solve my problem of lunch with Simon.

The morning passed in a hurried rush for Adrian. It seemed as though everyone in Savannah had suddenly discovered a need for temporary help. Even as Sara waved good-bye on her way out, Adrian was on the phone with yet another customer. By the time she'd reassured a Mr. Johnston that someone would be at his store the following morning to fill in for an employee who was ill, she was ready for a break.

Adrian dialed Smitty's and ordered a ham and cheese on rye, then walked over to the small table in one corner of her office and poured herself a cup of coffee. If business kept picking up, she mused as she added sugar and stirred, she'd be able to pay off her bank loan sooner than she'd first anticipated.

"And that, my dear, will make you master of all you survey!" she delivered dramatically, her free arm making a wide sweeping motion. "Or should it be mistress of all you survey? Oh, well, whatever, it will be mine, all mine."

The sound of someone clearing his throat in a rather pointed manner caused Adrian to freeze in her tracks. She had a horrible suspicion she knew precisely who her visitor was even before she looked.

With very controlled movements she set the cup of coffee on her desk and turned. "Didn't Mrs. Sorres give you my message?" she asked, a scowl pulling at her features.

It wasn't fair, she was thinking even as she was speaking, for any man to be so darned attractive. Simon was still standing in the doorway, his forearms and palms braced against the frame. He was impeccably dressed in a dark gray suit, a neatly striped tie, and a white shirt. But even in the perfectly tailored uniform of the successful executive, Adri-

51

an had an idea he'd be much happier in faded denims and a worn shirt.

"Well?" she demanded archly. "Did Mrs. Sorres tell you I couldn't make lunch?"

"Mrs. Sorres, the excellent secretary she seems to be, most certainly did inform me that Miss Kohl would be unavailable for lunch." Simon spoke in that annoying manner she was beginning to recognize as plain stubbornness.

"Didn't you believe her?"

"Mrs. Sorres, yes. You, no," he bluntly replied.

"Why on earth would I lie?" Adrian asked, deciding her best defense was to bluff.

"Because you're a coward, Adrian. Beautiful and charming, but nevertheless a coward. Why else would you allow yourself to remain engaged to a man you don't love?" He pushed away from the door and began walking toward her.

Adrian didn't bother protesting the unfairness of what he'd said. Partly because there was some truth in it—at least about her being a coward, that is—the other reason being her inability to think properly when being stalked. For at that precise moment every move of his powerful body, even his gaze through slitted lids, left her with the helpless feeling of the prey being cornered by the predator.

His forward progress ended, and all else was blocked from Adrian's view save a broad chest. When she made no move to change the situation by looking at him, Simon slipped a hand beneath her chin and forced her head up, his thumb lightly stroking her bottom lip.

"Did you really think I'd be put off by some half-baked scheme? That I'd simply give up and quietly fade into the woodwork like some docile puppy?"

The image his description conjured up brought a smile to her lips. "I'd hardly classify you as docile," Adrian murmured. "As to your other question, I'm not sure. I have a feeling this is all old hat to you. But there's another person involved, Simon, and I have no intention of being part of a triangle."

"Ah, now I understand," he smiled. "You think I want a quick tumble in bed and then good-bye. Right?"

Adrian lifted one slim shoulder. "Crudely put, but true. And, in spite of your opinion, I do love Jason."

Suddenly there was a brilliant fire in his eyes. The muscles in his face became taut and strained. "You do believe in tempting fate, don't you, Adrian?" he whispered as he reached for her.

Adrian braced herself for the first moment of contact, thinking of how she might protect herself. But any protection she may have constructed was swept away like a fragile flower being swamped by a tidal wave.

His tongue stormed the softness of her mouth, exciting her with its flaming tip as it sought out the gentle sweetness of her response.

For respond she did, like the first curling fingers of a new day's sun caressing the dew-kissed fragileness of a scented rose. She felt the velvety petals of her body slowly unfolding, being drawn upward and outward to the warmth that surrounded her.

It was two sharp rings of the telephone and then

silence when the caller evidently changed his mind and hung up that finally broke the two apart. But even then Simon was in no hurry to release her.

He slowly raised his head and stared down at Adrian. "You do know you're the world's biggest liar, don't you?" He whispered the question. He raised one hand to push back the wispy tendrils of hair that had fallen over her forehead.

"My plans are already made, Simon," she managed in a voice that sounded as though it belonged to someone else.

"Remember what they say about the best laid plans of mice and men, Adrian?"

"Being neither a man nor a mouse, I refuse to consider the metaphor," she countered with a touch of a smile pulling at her mouth.

"Then you've just made the biggest mistake of your life, sweetheart. And don't say I didn't warn you." There was such a glowing intensity in his dark eyes, it caused a quiver of anticipation to warm the blood in her veins.

Simon was practically a stranger. Yet she'd responded to him in a way she'd never done with Jason, and that stung.

With as much grace as she could muster, Adrian forced herself to step back from Simon, the scent of him making her giddy.

"How long have you been wearing Lang's ring, Adrian?" He broke the uneasy silence.

She reached for the coffee she'd poured earlier. "Almost a year." Her voice was soft and shaky. She took a sip of the dark brew, frantically searching her mind for something to say.

"During that time you've never wanted to set a definite date?" Simon asked in a disbelieving tone as he leaned against the edge of the desk and watched her.

"I believe in long engagements. It's a southern tradition," she said, watching him over the rim of her cup. "Is that a crime?"

"In your particular case I'd say no."

"Really? Then we have finally agreed on something." She was more relaxed now that there were a few feet separating them. She couldn't explain it nor did she want even to try. But in the shortest time possible, Simon Lord had swept into her life and was doing his darnedest to upset her well-ordered lifestyle. Something had to be done about the man before he became more of a disruptive influence.

"In case you haven't noticed, my secretary is out. I really can't leave the office," she explained, trying for a calm, matter-of-fact air.

"I know. That's why we're eating here," Simon told her, completely surprising her by the revelation. He looked at his watch. "Our lunch should be here in approximately four minutes. I hope you like crab salad."

Adrian simply stared at him, then sighed. "Unfortunately, it's one of my favorites." She walked around him and set her cup down on the desk and began clearing a space. "I hope you remembered rolls. I have an absolute passion for crisp, buttery rolls," she threw over her shoulder as she worked.

"The crispiest," Simon chuckled. "There's also cheesecake for dessert."

"Are you attempting to ply me with food and then seduce me?" Adrian asked with a resurgence of her former sense of humor as she stared at him across the width of the desk.

"Would it work?"

"No," she grinned. "But for one tiny moment the thought of a wealthy tycoon going to the trouble of having a tasty lunch prepared and sent up went to my head. I'm not sure I can handle Smitty's Sandwich Shop after today."

"Then I'll have to make a point of feeding you every day. Otherwise you might blow away."

Adrian's brow furrowed as she considered his remark. She glanced down at her figure and then at Simon. "Does your taste run to the more, er, voluptuous types? Strange," she mused. "I know we don't know each other very well, but I'd never have taken you for a fat freak."

"What the hell is a fat freak?" Simon scowled.

"You know. A man who's turned on by women of very generous proportions," she explained, almost unable to keep from laughing at his disgruntled expression.

"What would you say if I told you that you turn me on, Adrian Kohl?" The enigmatic expression in his eyes revealed nothing.

"Why, Simon." She smiled mischievously. "I'd congratulate you on your good taste and promptly forget it. I'd also be very disappointed. That line has been rather overdone, don't you agree?"

"Impudent little baggage, aren't you?" Simon quipped sourly, obviously displeased by her less than enthusiastic response to his efforts to get to know her better.

Whatever Adrian might have replied to his querulous remark was interrupted by the arrival of their lunch. She watched with wry amusement as the impassive-faced young man unpacked the specially insulated box. After checking each container of food, and satisfying himself that everything was in order, the waiter stepped back and looked at Simon.

"You've done your usual fine job, Sam," Simon drawled. He slipped one hand in his pocket and palmed a bill, which he transferred to the smiling waiter with such finesse, Adrian wondered just how many times Simon had acted out this particular little charade.

After Sam's departure Simon seated Adrian and pulled up the remaining chair for himself. With a command that came from years of giving orders and having them obeyed, he served their plates. Adrian looked skeptically at the huge portions he placed before her.

"Aren't you overdoing it just a bit?" she asked.

"In what way? By serving you your plate?" he coolly asked. "I don't think so. I enjoy doing things for certain people, Adrian. Especially gorgeous redheads with blue eyes.

"I wasn't referring to your, er, generosity, Simon,

and you know it," she explained. "Problem is, if I eat everything on my plate I'll have to take a nap." She grinned. "I happen to be one of those uncomplicated souls who gets sleepy after eating a huge meal."

"Mmm." Simon glanced about the small office and the minimal furnishings. "Next time we'll have to do this at my office." He looked directly at Adrian. "It would be very pleasant to watch you sleep after we've made love."

"Since there's no chance of that ever happening, I'd say it's a moot point, wouldn't you?" Adrian calmly countered between bits of the delicious crab salad. "Besides, Simon, you're too forceful for me. Being made love to by you would be comparable to being adrift in a hurricane. Thanks, but I think I'll stay with Jason. He's much safer."

Rather than being angered by her blunt honesty, Simon threw back his head and roared with laughter. Adrian continued to eat, unaware that her refreshing candor was far more appealing than the usual response Simon got from the women he knew.

"Are you usually as frank with the other men in your life?" he finally asked when he could talk again.

Adrian looked steadily at him across the desk, a decided frown touching the smoothness of her forehead. "There are no *other men* in my life, Simon. Only one, my fiancé. Why can't you accept that?"

"Because I don't choose to, Adrian," he answered without the slightest hesitation. "You're a beautiful, warm, and charming woman, all of which is wasted on Jason Lang. He's been spoiled and pampered by his mother, and he'll merely replace her by marrying you. You deserve better."

"Butt out, Simon," Adrian retorted without batting an eye. He was encroaching on territory where he had no right to be. "Jason is a warm and sensitive man, whom I happen to love. Furthermore," she went on as she broke a crusty roll in half, "I don't recall asking your advice regarding my personal life."

Simon sat back in his chair, a gleaming admiration reflected in his dark eyes. "It sounds good, honey. Loyalty, proclaiming your love—all the things one would expect from a happily engaged woman. But I know differently, don't I, Adrian? I've seen the tears in your eyes, remember? I've also held you in my arms and felt you respond to my kisses, my caresses."

Suddenly the excellently prepared lunch became as tasteless as sawdust to Adrian. She, too, sat back, her friendly mood replaced by one of confusion. "Why are you persisting with this insane idea?" she finally asked. She knew that everything he'd said was merely a repeat of her own thoughts of late. But she didn't want to hear it. Simon could never begin to understand someone as sensitive as Jason. Permanently away from Stella, Jason just might be an entirely different person. At least she owed him that much of a chance.

"Can you deny that you're attracted to me, Adrian?" Simon broke into her sad, almost painful reflections.

"No, I can't deny it." Her gaze narrowed. "I also

adore chocolate, but I'm forced to leave it alone. It gives me a rash."

"Believe me, Adrian. What you'll get from our relationship will be much more enjoyable than a rash," Simon chuckled throatily.

CHAPTER FOUR

"I'm sorry I was so late in getting back from lunch," Sara apologized during a break in the busy afternoon. "But Mark's mother insisted that we do some shopping."

"Don't worry," Adrian quickly reassured the receptionist. "I, er, accomplished quite a bit while you were out."

"You did?" Sara asked skeptically, looking at the large stack of work that had been on Adrian's desk since early morning. If anything, it seemed as if the pile had grown. "Did Smitty fix you one of his specialties?"

"Yes—I mean no," Adrian stuttered and then suffered the ignominy of a pink flush slowly stealing over her face. She then scolded herself for behaving so ridiculously. "Actually, I did have a delicious lunch, but it didn't come from Smitty's," she confessed somewhat ruefully.

"Oh? Tell me more." Sara immediately sat down, her undivided attention on her friend. "I'm all ears."

Why not? Adrian thought. Sara was level-headed as well as being able to keep things to herself. It would be interesting to see what her reaction was to Simon Lord's bizarre behavior.

"As you will recall, last night Jason and I went to Sandra's party." At Sara's nod, Adrian continued. "Also at the party was Simon Lord."

"Oh, dear. Was he still breathing fire?"

"No. In fact, he was so pleasant I was sure there'd been some dreadful mistake. Especially after having endured his nasty temper for the entire afternoon. However, he went out of his way to redeem himself. He even asked me to lunch," she finished on a light note, omitting the more intimate moments of her last two encounters with Simon.

Sara sat back in her chair, a surprised look on her face. "I'm impressed. From the amount of trouble he's given us I would have been more inclined to think of him ruining your lunch rather than providing it."

"So would I. But, I'll have you know, our Mr. Lord doesn't do anything by half measure, my dear. I was feted to crab salad, crisp rolls, and cheesecake. How does that strike your fancy?" Adrian grinned cheekily.

"I think it's fantastic. Better still, how does it strike you?" Sara asked. "Seems to me the gentleman went to a lot of trouble to make amends." She was

62

quiet for a moment. "He knows you're engaged," she murmured thoughtfully. "Seems to me Mr. Lord is more than a little anxious to make up for his horrid manners. I wonder why?" she asked with a mischievous twinkle in her eyes.

"I really didn't bother to question his motives, Sara," Adrian lied glibly. "But I certainly did enjoy his food. Now," she said, switching the conversation to safer ground, "how's it coming with Mark's mother?"

"Great. She's really nice. It's a shame she doesn't have a daughter. Although she's quite proud of her sons, all five of them."

"Don't quibble with your good fortune. The lady knows you and Mark are planning a spring wedding. She'll have her daughter then," Adrian smiled.

"I suppose you're right. Speaking of future mothers-in-law, has the cold war between you and Stella Lang let up?" Sara asked. She was aware of the antagonistic attitude of the older woman toward Adrian and felt comfortable enough to ask the question.

"I think war is the operative word, sweetie. More often than I care to admit, I get an almost uncontrollable urge to choke that charming lady," Adrian confessed.

"I'm sorry. It's been almost a year. You would think she'd have given up by now and accepted the fact that you and Jason are getting married."

"Stella reminds me of an elephant, Sara. Forgetting isn't in her makeup. Her latest little trick is that we should move in with her."

"Don't do it," Sara advised. "We've both seen what happens—disaster. Have you given Jason your decision?"

"Oh, yes. Immediately after he mentioned it. He's still sure I'll change my mind though."

In fact it was the first thing Jason asked her upon arriving at her apartment later that evening.

"I'm ready on time for a change," Adrian smiled as she let him in. "I decided I'd surprise you."

"Don't tell me your business is so slow you can leave when you want," he teased. He reached out and pulled her to him, kissing her warmly.

"Indeed not," she boasted somewhat proudly. "I'm even hoping to pay off my loan before it's due. What do you think of that?"

"I think that with our combined incomes, plus not having to pay rent by living with Mother, I can add to my law library as well as invest in that office computer system I've had my eye on."

Adrian's mood was immediately darkened, the sparkling light leaving her blue eyes. She moved out of the circle of his arms. "I thought I made it clear to you last night, Jason. I have no intention of moving in with your mother."

"Oh, honey," he sighed. "Please do this one small thing for me. It will make things so much easier. I'll have you, and it'll keep Mother happy."

"It may come as a surprise to you, Jason, but keeping your mother happy at the expense of our happiness hardly fills my heart with warmth," Adrian said in a cool voice. "In case you've forgotten, I was raised in an atmosphere that was sadly lacking in privacy. I've no intention of deliberately thrusting myself back into the same situation just so you can pacify Stella."

Jason walked over and stared at the collection of records and tapes in the lower shelf of a large bookcase, the fingers of one hand idly flipping through the upright jackets. "You sound hostile, Adrian."

"I think adamant is the better word, Jason. I refuse to be manipulated by your mother. I'm hoping you'll break the news to her without me having to get involved."

"I suppose I'll have to, won't I?" he answered defiantly. When he turned, Adrian could see his petulant expression, the downward pull of his mouth. "I was really counting on you," he said accusingly.

Adrian tipped her head to one side and shrugged. "I learned long ago to count as little as possible on other people's help in attaining the things I want from life, Jason. Perhaps you should do the same."

All during the ride to the restaurant where they were meeting Jason's colleague, John Roach, and his date for dinner, she was aware of the tension between them. She tried several times to include Jason in the conversation with John and Amy, but Jason, by his short, curt responses, let her know that he was still annoyed and that he was punishing her by his frigid silence.

He's probably thinking I'll give in, Adrian thought as she finally stopped all efforts to draw him out of his dark mood, *but I won't. Moving in with Stella Lang is the most unappealing thing I've ever faced.*

They were midway through dinner before Jason showed any signs of thawing toward Adrian. He'd sulked like a small boy and she had left him with it, talking and laughing with John and Amy.

If John was aware of his colleague's frosty manner, he conveniently ignored it. He was relating a particularly amusing incident to the two women when he happened to glance past Jason toward the entrance of the dining room.

"Well, well. I see Simon Lord has just come in. Aren't you doing some work for him, Jason?"

"Simon? Here?" Jason came to life as if someone had suddenly turned on a light inside his head. He threw a quick look over his shoulder and then shrugged. "I've done a few things. Can you imagine the lucky stiff that will eventually get his business locally?"

"I know what you mean," John concurred. "The retainer would be very nice . . . very nice indeed."

"Honestly." Adrian gave a huge sigh of disgust that hid the quivering within her at the sight of Simon. "First Jason and now you, John. What's so important about handling Simon Lord's business? There are other firms, other people in Savannah who are just as important. And since neither of you is exactly starving, I find this importance you've tagged him with to be a bit ridiculous."

Both men openly scoffed at her disdainful attitude and Adrian accepted their disfavor without further argument. Why bother pointing out to Jason that he was presenting himself in a less than favorable light? Worse still was the fact that Simon Lord could see through the younger man without the slightest effort. He'd made his fortune by correctly reading people. Unfortunately Jason presented no more of a challenge than a ten-year-old.

Under cover of the conversation going on around her, Adrian found herself watching Simon's progress as he and the two men he was with were shown to a table close to where Adrian and her party were sitting.

Knowing that any moment he was going to look up and see her watching him, she told herself to stop staring. But before the command could be carried out, she found herself looking straight into a pair of dark brown eyes.

At first there was a flicker of surprise in his gaze, but it was swiftly replaced by outright pleasure. Unable to tear her eyes away, Adrian witnessed the transformation of his harsh features into a pleasant smile. His brief but definite nod of greeting brought an acknowledgment in kind from Adrian without her even being aware of having done so.

There was a purpose in his smoldering look, a language that Adrian would have had to be blind not to see. The overriding message—I want you. The depth of his desire ignited in Adrian a deep, intense warmth that slowly spread outward through her body to the very tips of her fingers and toes.

Had anyone chosen that precise moment to look at the two people locked in a pulsating awareness of each other, they would have been stunned, so great was the force coursing between the two.

Finally, it was John who drew Adrian's attention back to the people at her table.

"I'm sorry, John. What did you say?" she asked in startled confusion.

"I was just remarking that even though you're quick to put Jason and me down for going after Simon Lord's business, you've certainly benefited from his arrival."

"Oh, well," she grinned at his good-natured ribbing. "Some of us have it and some don't. Are you jealous?"

"Yes," he replied so honestly that they all were overcome by laughter.

It proved most difficult for Adrian to carry on an intelligent conversation when all the time she could feel Simon's eyes on her, watching, assessing. She finally gave up all pretense of finishing her dinner and refused dessert.

Suddenly she saw Simon and his companions rise, and her heart stopped. He was leaving. She was unable to account for the desolation that swept over her. He was upsetting, blunt, and arrogant, but he was also exciting and she would have been deceiving herself to have admitted otherwise.

Just when Adrian knew Simon would turn and follow his friends, he stopped, his gaze narrowing at the unwitting longing he saw reflected in her eyes.

With something akin to an explosion of stars bursting in her veins, she watched him take his first step toward her table. She leaned heavily back in her chair, her relief so intense she felt her body shudder with weakness.

"Hello, Jason, John, ladies." Simon spoke in that perfectly modulated voice she'd come to know so well. He paused between John and Jason, including Adrian in his encompassing glance, seeming to know that she needed time to compose herself.

"Simon!" Jason exclaimed as he rose to his feet, his hand outstretched. Introductions to Amy were made. "Would you join us for dessert? Coffee?" Jason asked, his overwhelming awe as well as his innate graciousness prompting the invitation.

"If I wouldn't be intruding, coffee sounds nice." But rather than taking Jason's chair that he eagerly offered, Simon deftly stepped around him and borrowed one from another table and placed it between Jason and Adrian.

It was done so casually, so smoothly, that only Adrian was aware of the real reason behind his move.

She made no attempt to enter into the conversation. If she did, Simon would be sure to give her his full attention and she didn't want that. This excitement he created in her was too new to be dealt with in public.

But after chatting with Jason and John, and after totally disarming Amy, Simon did turn to Adrian, and she felt the momentary brush of his hard thigh against her own.

"No dessert, Adrian? I had the cheesecake and it was delicious. In fact, I've had cheesecake twice today," he gently taunted as his eyes swept over her, then lingered on the revealing neckline of the soft green dress she was wearing and the shadowed hollow between her creamy breasts.

Adrian could feel her fingers slowly curling until both hands were tightly clenched beneath the table. *Don't do this to me,* she wanted to cry out. *Don't turn this . . . this feeling I have for you into a contest between you and Jason. This belongs to me and I'll allow no one to tamper with it.*

"How nice for you," she said without revealing the depth of the emotion flooding within her. "Aren't you afraid of becoming bored with a steady diet of the same thing? I know I would. I like variety. You should be more daring, Simon. Savannah is noted for its cuisine." The play on words brought a gleam of mischief to brown pools that were caressing her like a brush of soft velvet against her heated skin.

"Variety, hmmm?" He spoke for her ears only. "I'll remind you of that in the very near future." He chuckled at the embarrassing blush that flowed over her face. He turned and put some question to Jason, who was more than a little annoyed that his fiancée would treat someone as important as Simon Lord so casually, not to mention that he was unable to hear all they were saying.

Jason began an all-out effort to swing the conversation around to the economy and the positive affect Lord Electronics would have on Savannah's job force.

After that, Adrian became an interested listener, speaking only when a remark was directed to her. She didn't feel left out. It was rather heady to be able to sit and observe Simon.

His mouth held a special fascination for her, her thoughts going back to the evening before, to mere

70

hours ago at noon, and his lips taking hers and the unbelievable way she'd responded.

She could still feel the strength of his arms around her, the slightly abrasive stroke of his hands. Oh, yes, she reminded herself, watching Simon Lord could become a most addictive habit.

Her thoughtful rumination was abruptly shattered by Simon, and in a manner that had Adrian longing to choke him.

"Jason, I need to ask a favor of you," he began in a pleasant voice.

"Anything at all, Simon," Jason offered.

"Since Adrian has been helping me with my office staff, several points have arisen that I need to discuss with her. Since both our schedules are so hectic, I would like your permission to take your fiancée to lunch. So far, she's been most reluctant to be seen with me."

Oh, you ass! Adrian was tempted to shout at him and his slick maneuver. It took untold self-control for her not to gape like some surprised idiot at this blatant lie. Even more humilating was Jason's accusing look before he assured Simon that Adrian was free to see him anytime.

Simon turned to her, such a solicitous expression of concern on his face that only Adrian could see the triumphant gleam in his eyes. "See, I told you Jason would understand."

"Yes," Adrian murmured, barely able to control her rage. "I can see that you were correct." With a hand that wasn't quite steady she lifted her wineglass

71

to her lips in the hope that the contents would help calm the sudden ache in her heart.

On the way back to her apartment Adrian decided to take another stab at making Jason see that Simon wasn't anything special. For with all his weird little quirks, Jason was a gentle person and she didn't like to see him humbling himself for anyone.

"I wish you hadn't interfered when Simon asked your permission to take me to lunch, Jason," she used as an opener. "I have other clients who are considerably less trouble."

He laughed easily, his mood vastly improved. "He really gets to you, doesn't he?"

"Yes," Adrian managed, privately thinking it to be the understatement of the year. "But, more than that, I resent this . . . this everything-at-all-costs attitude you and John accord the man."

"Well, from that aspect I'm afraid you and I have different views. As for giving him my permission . . ." Jason grinned. "We all know he was roasting you."

"You really don't mind if I have lunch with him, even dinner?" Adrian persisted. At his unconcerned "Of course not," she inwardly groaned. She wasn't sure why she was belaboring the point . . . or was she? Did she want Jason to tell her in no uncertain terms to stay clear of Simon Lord? Hadn't she wanted him to look Simon straight in the eye and tell him that any business Simon had with Adrian would have to be done during business hours?

The questions had been asked, but the answers

weren't at all what she wanted to hear. For Jason had done none of those things. He'd simply agreed with Simon, and Simon knew that Jason was nothing more than a minor nuisance in his pursuit of Adrian.

She glanced at Jason's pleasing profile. What was there about him that made her feel that she had to protect him? It was as though she were waiting for some mysterious metamorphosis to take place in him, after which he'd become the stronger of the two and she could lean on him. But would that ever happen?

CHAPTER FIVE

From the moment Adrian was awakened by the strident buzzing of her alarm clock, her mind was flooded with thoughts of Simon Lord.

All during the time it took her to dress and drive to her office she was trying to figure out ways to avoid him. He was devastatingly attractive, but she knew that if she didn't stop him, he was sure to cause her heartache.

Already she'd learned that Simon was a law unto himself. Adrian could easily see how a man in his position could become so wrapped up in the complicated workings of his corporation that the more tender emotions and concerns would be lost.

Engagements, marriages, commitments from a woman to a man, obviously weren't very high on his list of priorities. He'd proved that by choosing to ignore Jason's rightful place as her fiancé.

74

And that, she reminded herself while she parked her old-model VW in the parking lot behind her office, is reason enough to stay away from the man. But she found herself thinking, *he's intriguing and he's also the most exciting man I've ever met. Why couldn't he have happened at another time in my life?*

"Good morning." Sara smiled cheerfully as her boss entered the small but attractive reception area.

"That's debatable," Adrian groaned. She eyed the mug of steaming coffee sitting on the desk. "Ah . . . that smells good."

"Er, did you have a late night?" Sara asked, following Adrian into her office. She was beginning to be more than a little curious by the mysterious insomnia that had suddenly assailed her friend. It simply wasn't Adrian.

"Twelve or so," Adrian threw over her shoulder after dropping her purse and heading straight for the coffee. "You know me. I'm the original night owl. It's not the late hours," she said as she stirred her coffee. "I seem to have suddenly become unable to sleep."

She didn't bother to explain that every time she closed her eyes she was haunted by Simon Lord's face, followed by pangs of guilt that it wasn't Jason who dominated her thoughts. Even when she was finally able to drift off to sleep, the two men wrecked that supposedly peaceful period.

There would be Simon, exciting and sexy, beckoning her to him. The closer she got, the more mocking his expression became. Then there was Jason, alternately accusing and pleading, his image merging confusedly from that of a small boy to a man, with Adrian unable to separate the two.

"Is there something wrong with the business that I don't know about?" Sara asked.

"Oh, no," Adrian assured her. "Business is fantastic." She walked back to her desk and sat down. "Things just seem to be piling up on me." She sighed. "Perhaps I'm at one of those low points people are always talking about."

"Maybe so." Sara didn't press the issue. If and when Adrian was ready to talk, she'd listen. Otherwise she wouldn't interfere. They were good friends, but they also respected each other's privacy.

"By the way," Adrian said as Sara started to leave the room. "If Simon Lord calls, tell him I'm out . . . busy . . . whatever comes to mind. I don't want to talk with him."

"Don't worry, I'll handle him," Sara assured her.

Handle Simon? Adrian was tempted to laugh outright at such a remark. One should be so lucky. She seriously doubted that anyone had ever successfully handled Simon in their entire life.

Contrary to the ever-present thought of having to deal with her tormentor, Adrian didn't hear from Simon at all during the day.

Lunch came and went without incident. It was well into the afternoon when it dawned on her that instead of feeling overwhelming relief, there was a taste of disappointment, which only served to annoy Adrian and resulted in her giving herself a stern lecture.

It was during this lengthy chastisement that Jason

76

called, his voice excited as he told her that Simon Lord had hired him to take care of some additional legal work.

"That's great, Jason," she replied warmly. "I know how much you've wanted that chance." She meant it. Jason was an excellent attorney and deserved the opportunity Simon was offering. Her only reservation was that Simon had done the offering.

That aspect of the situation wasn't so easily accepted. For it meant his continued influence in their lives, an influence Jason was too blind to see.

"There's only one catch, honey," Jason ran on, jolting Adrian back to his enthusiastic chattering. "I'll have to be away a good deal of the time."

"Oh? Do you have any idea how long?" she asked.

"Not for weeks and weeks if that's what you're thinking," he chuckled. "Three or four days at a stretch should cover it. We'll be working with Simon's legal staff based in Denver. From what he told me, we'll be making trips to other branches of Lord Electronics as well."

"We?" Adrian asked. "You mean he hired John too?"

"No, no, John wasn't hired. Simon has a young executives' program. One phase of their training is that each participant see the business from every angle. The newest trainee will be doing some traveling with me."

"Sounds interesting enough. But what about your own practice?"

"Most of my cases are set for the next term of

court. Anything else that comes up can be handled by John. This is too great an opportunity to let pass, Adrian," he pointed out in a slightly defensive tone.

"I'm sure it is, Jason. I only wish you weren't going to be away so much. Have you told your mother the news?" In her mind's eye she could see Stella Lang's expression of horror at the thought of Jason being free from her domination.

"As a matter of fact I have. She was very pleased. I must admit I was surprised," he admitted.

It was only after they'd made plans for the evening and she had cradled the receiver that the full significance of Stella's reaction hit Adrian. It was obvious the older woman was hoping the separation would drive a wedge between the couple. She'd probably be just as happy to see him go to the North Pole, Adrian thought acidly as she tried to concentrate on her work.

With Stella and Simon attempting to sabotage her engagement, Adrian was beginning to be a bit apprehensive regarding the outcome.

The remainder of the afternoon passed quietly enough, but there was a nagging suspicion in Adrian's mind that Simon had deliberately given Jason work that would take him out of town.

Even after she'd left the office and gone home to shower and dress for her date with Jason, she found herself unable to believe Simon had acted unselfishly.

He'd expressed his opinion of her engagement and her fiancé to Adrian too many times for her to be taken in by such a slick tactic. *Oh, yes,* she told herself as she finished with her hair and makeup, then took a leaf-green colored dress from its hanger, *Mr. Lord is definitely up to no good. I only wish I could convince Jason of that fact.*

With a frown creasing her usually smooth forehead, Adrian stepped into the dress, drew the soft, silky material up over her body, then eased the zipper into place. It wasn't a new dress, but it was one of her favorites. The lines were simple and very flattering to her slimness.

After surveying her reflection in the full length mirror that was attached to the closet door, she gave a barely audible murmur of approval.

A couple of unnecessary strokes of the hairbrush to her hair, a quick check of her makeup, and Adrian was ready. Just as she reached for the small clutch bag and her wrap, the peal of the doorbell sounded.

She hurried to the door, hoping during the course of the evening to discourage Jason from accepting Simon's offer. It would be a difficult task, and one she wasn't looking forward to at all. How could she simply blurt out that Simon was much more interested in getting her into his bed and that Jason was less likely to interfere if he was safely out of the way?

Her apprehension was momentarily forgotten, however, when she admitted a beaming Jason. Before Adrian could do more than return his smile, she felt herself being swooped up in his arms and whirled about.

"I hope you've got your dancing shoes on, sweetheart, because after dinner we're going to do some celebrating." He grinned down at her as he set her back on her feet, his hands locked behind her back.

"You really are excited about this, aren't you?" She smiled. Deep in her heart she was happy for him, but the more practical side of her nature bled for this gentle, loving man and the trap he was rushing so blindly into.

"That, my dear Miss Kohl, is putting it mildly. I'm ecstatic! And"—he placed a forefinger against the softness of her lips—"I don't want to hear one word against Simon Lord. Understand?" At Adrian's bleak nod of agreement, he went on. "I know you don't care for the fellow, but I really think I'm making the right decision. Okay?"

"Okay," Adrian smiled in spite of herself. "But there's no law that says I have to look forward to being apart from you for days at a time."

"Are you saying that you'll miss me?" Jason warmly chuckled.

"Of course, you nut!"

"Then perhaps I have more to be grateful to Simon for than I realized. You know what they say about absence making the heart grow fonder. Maybe us being apart will spur you toward setting a definite date for our wedding."

"Ah." Adrian grinned teasingly. "Now I get the picture. All this going on about advancing your career has been nothing but a ploy. What you really want is an early wedding."

"Early, Adrian?" Jason gently murmured. "It's been almost a year now. Every time I've brought up the subject, you've found ten different reasons why we should wait. I'm beginning to think you really don't want to marry me at all."

"Of course I want to marry you," she protested.

"Then while I'm away why don't you decide on a date? I think I'd feel a lot more confident if I knew that on a certain day in the very near future you'd be Mrs. Jason Lang."

"I'll think about it, I promise," Adrian hedged. She was uncomfortable with being pressed to name a date, and again she wondered why.

All during dinner, as Jason explained the various aspects of his new position with Lord Electronics, Adrian listened with only half an ear. Not that her attention wasn't entirely devoted to her fiancé, because it was.

But for once she wasn't able to push back the spreading fingers of doubt that hovered just beneath the surface of her mind.

She watched Jason as though seeing him for the first time, his voice sounding almost like that of a stranger.

Instead of the overwhelming love and desire for him that should have warmed her heart, there was, instead, compassion, sympathy, and affection, and, yes, even love of a kind. All the qualities usually present in a deep friendship between two people, she reflected sadly.

Unnoticed by Jason, she eased back in her chair, her discovery leaving her with a hollow feeling that was devastating. She reached for her wineglass and raised it to her lips.

Fleeting memories from her childhood whipped through her thoughts as she recalled the number of times she had rushed into a fracas to rescue a younger, smaller child from one of the several bullies at the orphanage. *Unfortunately,* a tiny voice within her reasoned, *you've transferred those same protective instincts to Jason. You do love him, but . . .*

Again there was a quiet thoughtfulness on Adrian's face as Jason continued with his enthusiastic chatter. She must have answered him at the appropriate times, and even managed to eat several bites of the delicious stuffed eggplant with crab meat dressing without arousing his suspicions.

Inwardly her thoughts were embroiled in a tangled mesh of confusion. Could she handle marriage with Jason? Worse still, was her concern for him genuine? Hurting him was something she simply couldn't do.

When the maddening swirl of her thoughts threatened to swamp her, Adrian excused herself and hurried to the ladies' room. Once inside the tastefully decorated room, she crossed over to the huge mirror that spanned the wall facing the door and sat down on one of the blue velvet-cushioned chairs.

A deep sigh rushed past her lips as she propped her chin on her palms and stared at her reflection. Jason would be leaving the next day, and when he returned he wanted a definite date for their wedding.

Adrian felt as though she were being torn in half. Jason was pressing on one side, and Simon Lord had wasted no time in totally undermining what she'd previously considered to be her neatly ordered life. In the wings there was Stella, adding her poison to the cauldron of indecision that had begun to take over Adrian's life.

Several minutes went by before she made any

effort to apply fresh lipstick, and she only did so then because two women had entered the room and were casting curious glances her way.

With a smile that was forced and a determined squaring of her shoulders, she reached for the doorknob.

She was halfway across the dining room before she looked toward Jason. When she did, she stopped dead in her tracks. He was no longer alone, but had been joined by Simon Lord and an attractive blonde, who was quite stunning in a black sequined affair!

Adrian's first impulse was to turn and run. She didn't want to see Simon. Since meeting him hardly a day had gone by without him touching her life in some way. And thus far his meddling had proved disastrous for her peace of mind.

Common sense prevailed, however, and Adrian found herself walking toward the cozy threesome with a thin smile touching her attractive mouth.

As she approached the table, Jason and Simon rose to their feet. There was a slight flush staining Jason's blond features that had Adrian staring curiously at him.

"So you did decide to return. I'd begun to think you'd deserted me," he laughed a bit nervously as he pulled out her chair and held it. "I'd like you to meet Janelle Kroft, Adrian. Janelle, this is my fiancée, Adrian Kohl."

Up close, Janelle Kroft was even more beautiful than Adrian had first thought. With a determination that wasn't lost on the remaining party of the foursome, Adrian deliberately began a conversation with the blonde and continued it for several minutes. When she was eventually forced to look at Simon, Adrian's hackles immediately rose at the knowing grin that pulled at his lips.

We're like puppets, she angrily thought, *and he's getting immense pleasure from pulling the strings.* The added discomfort of having him sitting to her right did little to soothe her troubled thoughts. His nearness and her own sensual awareness of him merely added to her mounting problems.

"How are you, Adrian?" Simon asked with just the proper degree of cordiality in his voice.

"Fine," she replied in as pleasant a tone as she could manage. Jason had immediately started talking to Janelle, and Adrian was left to Simon.

"I assume Jason has told you he'll be doing some work for me," Simon continued in that same polite manner that had Adrian itching to slap him. "Unfortunately, he'll have to be away part of the time. But I assured him I'd be available to escort you to any parties or pressing engagements that might crop up in his absence."

This time there was no hesitation in the burning gaze Adrian directed toward him. "How kind of you, Simon. But, in case you don't know, I grew up in Savannah. Maybe, just maybe, I could manage to scrape up an escort if I need one. I'm sure you've more pressing things to do than to fill in for Jason."

"You're too modest, Miss Kohl," Simon said softly. "What could possibly be more important than escorting a beautiful woman? By the way, if I were you, I'd make Janelle promise to keep a sharp eye on Jason."

"That would be an admirable feat, wouldn't it? Considering the fact that he'll be in Denver while she's here in Savannah, I fail to see the connection."

"Tsk, tsk." Simon tried for the stricken look and failed miserably. "I see that I've spoken out of turn. Forget I mentioned it." He leaned back in his chair, his dark brows arched in feigned contrition at his supposed faux pas.

Adrian looked from him to Jason, still in deep conversation with Janelle Kroft. For two people meeting for the first time they certainly seemed to have a lot to say to each other.

Unwittingly, her eyes were drawn back to Simon, who was sitting and observing the two blond heads huddled close together with a certain smugness that caused a suspicious glitter to appear in the smoldering depths of Adrian's eyes. "Just what am I supposed to forget?"

For a fraction of a second Adrian thought she detected a touch of pity in Simon's enigmatic stare, but he blinked his eyes so quickly, Adrian was sure she must have imagined it.

He leaned toward her, his harsh features noticeably gentle. "Janelle will be traveling with Jason. I honestly thought he'd told you," he said, noting the look of genuine surprise that rushed to her face on hearing the news.

"How . . . nice," she softly murmured. Inwardly she was seething. Now she knew the reason for Jason's uneasiness when she'd returned to the table. He hadn't planned on letting her know that Janelle was the young executive who would be accompanying him to Denver!

CHAPTER SIX

"Don't you think I'd rather have heard the news from you than Simon Lord?" Adrian asked angrily as Jason drove her back to her apartment. The space in the car was tense and electrified as their tempers flared.

Their plans for the evening had been ruined after Simon dropped his little bomb. The thought of dancing—for Jason was sure to have insisted that Simon and Janelle join them—was the furthest thing from Adrian's mind.

Earlier, as Simon told Adrian about Janelle, Jason had looked up and met Adrian's startled gaze.

Adrian, rather than letting Janelle know that Jason had conveniently omitted mentioning her, turned the tables on Jason by asking the attractive blonde if she was looking forward to the training program. She even went so far as to urge Janelle to

87

see that Jason took her to dinner in the evenings rather than working straight through till all hours.

All the while she was speaking, Adrian kept a charming smile glued to her face, acting for all the world as though it were the most natural thing in the world for her fiancé to be leaving the next morning with an attractive blonde.

Adrian chose to be pleasant even to Simon, determined to mask the rising anger that was coursing through her body like a river of molten lava, although she wasn't too sure whether or not he believed her softly spoken words or her forced charm.

By the time a relieved Jason—erroneously basking in Adrian's good graces—suggested that the four of them continue the evening by going dancing, Adrian surprised him with her firm refusal.

"After all, sweetheart, it will be our last evening together for several days," she offered sweetly, not missing the sudden clenching of Simon's fist that was resting on the edge of the table. "Since meeting Miss Kroft, I'm not about to let you go away without a proper sendoff." She positively beamed at the other two, playing to the hilt the role of a woman about to be separated from her lover.

"Oh . . . er . . ." Jason stammered, confused. "In that case we'd better be on our way. A guy doesn't get an offer like that every day." He rose to his feet and moved over to pull out Adrian's chair. "Janelle, I hope you'll excuse us. I'll see you at seven thirty sharp at the airport," he said in a jovial fashion. "Simon . . ." He extended his hand to his new boss, who had also risen. "I'll be in touch. I'm looking forward to this venture very much."

"Oh, yes, Simon," Adrian echoed Jason's ingratiating tone. "This evening's celebration will always be remembered as having come about due to your generosity. You've no idea how appreciative Jason will be in the morning," she smiled in spite of the icy blast emanating from Simon.

There was a distinct grayness around his mouth, a rigid tautness about his features as his burning gaze bored straight into Adrian's very soul.

She knew how angry he was, for she was suffering from the same affliction. She was purposefully letting both Simon and Janelle Kroft believe that Jason's last night before his departure would be spent in her arms.

"How sweet," Janelle chimed in before Simon could speak. "I know I'm going to enjoy working for Lord Electronics." Her eyes rested on Simon. "Everyone is like one big happy family."

Adrian was tempted to sink another two-edged knife into Simon's back but restrained herself. She was tired and angry and wanted nothing more than to get to her apartment.

Immediately after getting into the car, she turned on Jason, letting him know exactly how she felt about his deception.

"You're not exactly known for your rational thinking, you know," he retaliated, completely taken aback by her swift change from warm, inviting attentiveness to cold, hard fury. "Knowing how unreasonable you can be, I've been concerned since I told you, afraid you'd do something crazy."

"What, for heaven's sake?" she cried. "I'm impressed that you think I have such influence over Simon Lord." She laughed harshly. "Why, I snap my fingers and he drops whatever he's doing and comes running." She gave Jason a withering look and then turned and stared unseeingly out the car window.

"Now that I think back," Jason continued the battle, "I can see that everything you said and did after learning about Janelle was merely a ploy."

"How astute, Jason," she retorted sarcastically. "Had you rather I stand and applaud the fact that you lied to me? I felt like ten kinds of a fool when your esteemed employer let the cat out of the bag. And for your information, it was not an accident. He banked on you keeping silent about the curvaceous Miss Kroft."

"Really, Adrian," Jason replied in the most infuriating manner. "You sound as though the man is deliberately trying to separate us. I doubt if he gives either of us a thought beyond business."

"Oh?" she swiftly countered. "What if I told you that this fabulous opportunity he's given you is simply a means of getting you out of the way so that he can spend some time with me? What would you say to that?"

"That's easy," he calmly answered. "I'd say you are jealous. Jealous that I'll be away, and jealous that I'll be spending time with an attractive woman. It's not an uncommon emotion to feel, Adrian, but I hope in the future you'll be better able to control it."

At that moment Adrian realized she'd lost the war. No matter what she said, even to relating each of her encounters with Simon, and admitting to the strange attraction she felt for him, Jason wouldn't believe her.

She pushed back in her mind Jason's inability to see Simon for what he really was. Now wasn't the time to delve into Jason's strange reasoning. She was angry and would say and do things she would be sorry for later.

Perhaps the separation would be good for them. The disturbing thoughts she'd had earlier in the evening would have to be dealt with sooner or later. With him away it might prove an easier task.

There was a melancholy expression on Adrian's face as she sat at her desk. Jason had been away for three days and he'd called her only once. There'd been no mention of Janelle. He hadn't offered any information and Adrian hadn't asked about her. Their conversation had been strained and Adrian was relieved when it ended.

True to his word, Simon Lord had been most attentive in Jason's absence. So much so, Adrian was ready to scream. To her, it seemed he'd chosen her office as his favorite haunt. He even had Sara ready to do his slightest bidding.

"Leave!" Adrian had yelled at him on one particular instance when she'd looked up and found him in her office casually leaning against the wall staring at her. "This is a business office, not the local peep show."

"Do I bother you, Adrian?" he asked with a roguish grin on his face.

"Yes. It's a new experience, Simon. I've never been the object of lecherous ogling before," she snapped back at him.

"Lecherous ogling?" he laughed incredulously. "Please, keep your voice down. I do have a reputation to maintain, you know."

For several seconds Adrian continued to glare at him, but her sense of humor got the best of her and she found herself thawing toward him, a betraying smile replacing the scowl. "You're incorrigible." She pushed back the folder she'd been studying. "What do you want?"

"You."

"What's your second choice?" she asked without batting an eye.

"Have lunch with me. I'm hoping to wear down your defenses."

"You have only an hour. I doubt you're man enough to accomplish much in that length of time," she smiled sweetly and got to her feet.

"One day I'll surprise you, Adrian Kohl. Afterward you'll be mine forever."

She considered him thoughtfully, then said, "When that happens, Simon, you'd do well to bring your biggest guns, for I've no intention of giving in without a fight."

"Point taken, Miss Kohl."

"And so is five minutes of your hour," she answered cheekily.

* * *

Simon Lord. *Dear God,* she thought with an irritated shake of her head, *the man is driving me insane.* Adrian threw down the page on which were neatly typed columns of figures and swung her chair around to stare out the window.

The scene that greeted her wasn't particular uplifting due to the slow drizzle of rain that was threatening to become an all-day affair. The small courtyard around which her office, as well as several others, was situated looked as dismal and unappealing as she felt. The seasonal dropping of leaves from the trees and the bare starkness of the limbs gave the historical old city a gray, bleak appearance.

That morning, for the first time since she'd opened the doors of her business, Adrian had dreaded coming to work. She felt miserable, out of sorts, and she really couldn't put her finger on the reason for her unhappiness. Or could she?

Wasn't her problem the same one that had erupted so forcibly into her life only weeks ago? Hadn't part of her unhappiness arisen from the impossible task of trying to hate Simon Lord? "But I do hate him," she whispered to herself and the quietness of the room. "It's imperative that I do," she added, as though actually speaking the words aloud would help dispel the inexplicable hold he seemed to have over her.

He is a threat, she continued silently in her effort to expunge him from her mind. *A threat to my future and to Jason's.* Men like Simon literally feast on the weaker of their sex, mainly men like Jason.

But even with all the disquieting thoughts that ran rampant through the corridors of her mind, there was no way she could stop the image of Simon's face that swam before her eyes.

She thought back to before she met him, when he was only a deep, sometimes gravelly, always impatient voice on the telephone. She'd decided then that he must be an intolerable person, with an oversize ego. After meeting him face to face and withstanding that initial impact, she'd known differently. For whether or not she liked or approved of Simon, he had a certain charisma that appealed to her. There was a heady sensuality about him that stirred her in ways that left her breathless and unsure of herself.

When she'd been in his arms, Adrian had found warmth in the hardness of his body when she'd expected there to be coldness. His kisses had gently urged, then demanded a response that she'd never felt before. Later there had been a sadness in her heart that Jason had never evoked even a smattering of the response from her that she'd given so naturally to Simon.

The abrupt opening of the office door brought a startled Adrian back to the present. She swung around to her desk to see Sara hovering just inside, her lips compressed in rigid disapproval.

"Something wrong?" Adrian asked.

"You could say that," Sara grimaced. "Your future mother-in-law tried to barrel her way in and I stopped her."

It was all Adrian could do at that point to keep from laughing in spite of knowing who her visitor was. "Thank you, Sara. You can show her in now."

Once the humorous aspect was past, Adrian took

a deep breath and straightened her shoulders for the confrontation that was sure to come.

Suddenly the door opened and Stella Lang swept in. She was smartly dressed in a gray suit, and not a hair was out of place. Her makeup had been skillfully applied to hide or at lease minimize the lines of her fifty-odd years.

"Really, Adrian," she regally announced as she dropped her handbag on the desk and then sat down. "That young woman was terribly rude. I was appalled, simply appalled at the way she treated me, even after I told her who I was."

"I'm sorry, Stella. Sara is usually a friendly person. Perhaps she isn't feeling well today," Adrian pacified the older woman. She wasn't in the mood to exchange insults with Jason's mother.

"Was there something in particular you wanted to see me about?"

"Several things," Stella said without any warmth in her voice. "I'll get right to the point. Jason told me before he left that he's hoping you'll set a definite date for the wedding by the time he returns. Have you?"

Adrian stared a full ten seconds or so at the woman before answering. "Jason has only been away three days, Stella. But to answer your question, no, I haven't decided on a date."

"Well, at least that's a relief." She leaned back, her oval-tipped fingers tapping against the wooden arms of the chair. "Tell me, Adrian. Exactly what have you told my son about your childhood?"

"I beg your pardon?" Adrian frowned, wondering where on earth the conversation was headed.

"Your childhood." Stella waved one hand dismissively. "I find it odd that we know so little about you. After all, as Jason's wife there are certain organizations you'll be expected to join. You will have to supply them with several generations of your family tree."

"I'm afraid I won't be having time for club meetings, Stella," Adrian calmly replied. "I plan to continue working. I'm sure Jason's told you this."

"Well, of course he mentioned it, but I assumed you'd change your mind. Jason needs the contacts that can be made from your association with your bet . . . er . . . with people who are more influential than your present acquaintances," she coolly explained. "So, if you'll give me the names of your parents and go back, say, two or three generations, I think I can handle it from there."

"Thank you for wanting to help, but it won't be necessary," Adrian tried again for calmness. "I'm really not interested."

"Not interested? Or is it that you haven't the faintest idea who your ancestors were? That you have no idea who your parents were?" Stella reached for her handbag and opened it. Like a child delighted with a stocking on Christmas morning, she removed an official-looking document and handed it across to Adrian.

Without betraying the knot in her throat that was suddenly threatening to choke her, Adrian accepted the proffered paper and opened it. There was nothing new or revealing in the copy of her birth certificate, nothing that she hadn't seen time after time.

She scanned the contents, then looked at Stella. "Is there something I've missed? This is exactly the same as the one I have at home."

"You're very calm for an illegitimate nobody, I must say," Stella threw at her. All pretense of civility was wiped away, her expression was one of malicious glee. "Did you honestly think I'd stand by and let my son waste himself on the likes of you? You've set your sights too high, my dear. A Lang can hardly marry a nobody."

In spite of the trembling in her legs, Adrian rose to her feet so quickly Stella was startled. There was an overwhelming sense of pride in Adrian's blue eyes as she stared at the older woman. "Correction, Stella. I am somebody, and I don't need twelve or even three generations of my family tree to prove it. I know who and what I am; unfortunately, I can't say the same for you. If the truth were known, I'm sure the Langs knew some sad moments when they were forced to accept you into their family."

"Don't you dare speak to me that way!" Stella shrieked as she lunged to her feet. "As soon as I show Jason this piece of paper, you won't have to worry about a wedding date," she flung at Adrian.

"I wouldn't count on it, Stella."

"You wou . . ." Her face turned ashen. "Jason knows?"

"Oh, yes," said Adrian. "Since he first asked me to marry him. You see, Stella, unlike some people I know, I've never tried to be something I'm not. It's

97

called knowing who and what you are and being satisfied with yourself. Now"—she looked toward the door and back to her guest—"if you'll excuse me, I have a busy day ahead. By the way, shall I tell Jason that we've had this little talk?"

There was a deathly silence as the two women stared at each other. Finally Stella moved. She grabbed the single sheet of paper and stuffed it into her handbag. "You haven't won yet. I'll destroy you before I'll see my son married to you," she threatened in a menacing voice.

"Good-bye, Stella."

Without further exchange Stella turned and left the room, the unsteadiness of her steps seeming to belong to a much older woman.

Once the door closed, Adrian's veneer of calm began slowly to crumble. Gone was the poised, icy hauteur that had been present during her conversation with Stella. The tears spilled over and coursed crystal trails down her smooth cheeks. The knot in her throat had grown larger and was radiating an intense pain that was unbearable.

Without thought for the work on her desk, Adrian rushed over and grabbed the tan blazer she'd worn with her brown skirt and off-white blouse and hurried out of her office.

Sara looked up in confusion and half rose to her feet as Adrian dashed through the reception room. "Adrian? Adrian?" she called, only to have the door open and swing closed behind the slim figure who was oblivious to the sound of the human voice.

* * *

It all came rushing back to Adrian as she walked, the lonely dreams of a little girl. Dreams that one day she would be called into the office by the gently smiling nuns and told that her parents had come for her. Of course it never happened, but she never stopped dreaming, hoping.

The illegitimacy of her birth had been broken to her in such a kind fashion by the nuns who ran the orphanage that for a while afterward she really did believe she was very special—as they'd told her. But that bubble burst when she realized exactly what the word *illegitimate* meant.

It had become her secret then, the circumstances of her birth, with only the staff and later, Sandra, knowing. The only other person she'd ever told was Jason. By then the shame she'd felt had turned to a healthy acceptance of something she couldn't change.

Jason assured her that it didn't matter. He'd even joked and said that at least he wouldn't have to contend with a mother-in-law peering over his shoulder all the time. His casual acceptance of her birth had endeared him to her all the more.

Now Stella had found out. She'd said things to Adrian that she had secretly been afraid of for years. Things that wounded deeply, that cut into her very soul.

Her head was bowed against the rain, which was coming down in earnest now, but Adrian wasn't feeling the wetness. There was a numbness throughout her body that insulated her against the early fall temperature and the dampness. She was like a wounded animal, in pain but unable to find a safe corner to crawl into.

Suddenly there was a screech of tires from an automobile. Adrian heard the noise, but that was all. It simply failed to penetrate the thick fog of suffering surrounding her.

There were sounds of the car stopping, of quick, heavy footsteps and then the unyielding grip of a strong grasp on her arm. She looked down at the wide, tanned hand that seemed permanently attached to her arm and then at the face above the broad, dark-clad shoulders.

"Get in the car, Adrian," Simon gruffly directed her. There was a dead, vacant look in her eyes, her tears mingling with the rain.

She shook her head, finding it impossible to speak. Instead of taking her at her word, Simon simply swung her off her feet and hurried to his waiting car. Before Adrian could think, she was sitting in the front seat, with Simon behind the steering wheel.

"Here," he said in that same quiet voice as he shrugged out of his suit jacket. "Let's put this around you." He slipped limp arms into the sleeves and pulled the collar snug around her throat. "What's happened, sweetheart?" he asked worriedly. "Is it Jason?" But again Adrian merely stared at him.

Simon looked at her, noting the listlessness, the severe shock that had reduced her to this haunted, frightened person and softly cursed beneath his breath. Whoever or whatever had caused this trauma

Adrian was in would answer to him. Without further questioning he started the car and eased it into the line of traffic.

Whether it was the shock of suddenly being out of the rain and some of her body heat returning or Simon's forceful presence, Adrian wasn't sure. But she felt safe. The large scowling man beside her offered no threat. She'd found a safe haven in his arms before, and she was longing for that same soothing comfort again. She closed her eyes and gave in to the weariness that was enveloping her. Simon would take care of her.

"It's time to get out, Adrian," he said, jarring her out of the drowsy state she was drifting in. "Can you walk or do you want me to carry you?" Simon asked.

Time to get out? But it couldn't be, she reasoned. Her apartment was much farther away. She looked at the graceful lines of the town house that was obviously their destination. Was this where Simon lived? Apparently so. They were parked in a narrow drive and he seemed at ease.

"Adrian? Do you want me to carry you?"

"No, I'll walk," she managed. But when he opened the door and was hurrying her across a narrow patio toward a door she'd never seen, Adrian stumbled. Simon's strong arm about her waist immediately tightened as he ushered her forward and continued to hold her close while he unlocked the door.

"Is this your house?" Her voice sounded strange and distant even to her own ears.

"Yes," he returned smoothly. "I'd planned on

your seeing it, but not exactly under these conditions."

Without giving her time to do more than glance at the gleam of dark cupboards and the bright blue curtains at the windows, Adrian was whisked through the room, down a carpeted hall, through a bedroom, and into a bathroom.

In a flash Simon had the tub filling with water. Then he turned and began stripping the wet, soggy clothes from her body. His jacket, her blazer, skirt, and blouse were dealt with without regard to the delicacy of the fabric. When his hands reached for the front clasp of her bra, Adrian took an unsteady step backward, her hands pushing ineffectually at his much larger ones.

"Listen, sweetheart," Simon growled, his hands grasping her by the shoulders and giving her a short, quick shake. "At the moment you remind me of my favorite cat I had as a boy. He was always after the goldfish and always falling into the fishpond." He grinned. "I'll admit that you're put together a hell of a lot nicer than Fred, but at the moment I'm not interested. Okay?" There was a sureness, an intentness in his dark eyes that made Adrian know she could trust him.

Without further comment he completed undressing her. He turned off the water, then reached for a jar of bath salts, opened it, and dropped a generous handful into the steaming tub. Next he opened a louvered door and got out a large brown bath towel.

"Get in the tub, Adrian," he gently prodded. "When you've thawed out, slip into this." He held up a short navy velour robe. "It'll swallow you, but at least you'll be warm." With that he stared thoughtfully into her face and then walked out and closed the door behind him.

CHAPTER SEVEN

When Adrian emerged from the steaming bath a good thirty minutes later, she had Simon's robe wrapped and belted snugly about her body. She smiled at the comical size of the cuffs she had to make in order to free her hands of the long length of sleeve.

A shampoo had to be included before she could restore her hair to some semblance of order, and now a towel was wrapped turban-style around her head.

"I must say you resemble a mummy in that get-up," Simon drawled from the doorway of the master bedroom that adjoined the bath. He'd also changed, and wore dark trousers and a white long-sleeve sweater.

His casual dress and the manner in which it suited him held Adrian's attention far longer than she was aware of. There was something mezmerizingly fascinating about the smooth width of his shoulders, the way his broad chest tapered into a neat, trim waist. Without meaning to, her eyes followed the line of firm hips, hard, muscled thighs, and long legs. *Oh, my,* she silently mused in spite of her present misery, *I can just imagine the women flocking around him. No wonder he's never married. Why should he?*

"I don't believe I've ever been seduced before by a mere look." Simon spoke huskily from where he was still standing. "But now I'm learning that with the right person it can become rather heady."

A betraying flush stole over Adrian's features at having been so careless. "Don't confuse simple admiration for seduction, Simon," she remarked scowlingly. She raised her hands and began fiddling with the ends of the towel. "Surely you must know that you're a very attractive man."

"Ah." His brows shot up. "And all the while I thought you were lusting after my body. Oh, well," he sighed, "I suppose admiration is better than nothing. But was it my looks you were admiring or my act of mercy in rescuing you that brought about such an admission?" he teased.

"Neither," Adrian glibly lied as she gave him a level stare. "It was your sweater. I think I'd like one exactly like it—in a much smaller size, of course." *Now, Mr. Smarty Pants, let's see what you can make of that,* she thought.

"How would you like this one, Miss Kohl?" he gritted. "Preferably knotted around your beautiful neck?"

"Really, Simon. I'm shocked," she grinned in spite of herself.

"Then let me shock you further, you witch. If I ever catch you looking at me that way again, I definitely will not stop for conversation. Do I make myself clear?" His hooded expression gave Adrian cause to be very careful in answering.

"Of course," she meekly replied.

They continued the silent measuring of each other for several seconds and then Simon strode over and grabbed her by the hand. "Let's get the hell out of here before I throw you on that bed and make love to you," he ground out harshly.

Moments later Adrian was ensconced in one corner of a long sofa in a room that could be described only as masculine. She held a steaming mug of coffee laced with brandy between her hands and was staring dreamily into the fire Simon had started.

Oddly enough, she felt no embarrassment that he had undressed her—rather a sense of gratitude. He'd sensed her suffering and acted accordingly. Perhaps not as graciously or gallantly as some men, but his brusque treatment had been far more effective. It had been his concern for her that penetrated the numbness that Stella Lang's vicious attack had brought about.

For a moment there was a glitter of tears in her eyes. They were tears of anger and frustration that she'd allowed a person totally devoid of human feeling to cause her to lose control.

Adrian prided herself on her independence, her strength. And yet, in less time than she cared to think

106

about, Stella had turned her into someone momentarily incapable of rational thought. It was humiliating.

Simon's noisy entrance into the room brought a slight smile to her lips. As with everything else she'd seen him do, there was an aura of excitement surrounding him. Simon could never lead a quiet life.

"Feeling better?" he asked after the briefest of scrutinies before sprawling comfortably beside her on the sofa.

"Much better, thanks." Now that she'd regained her perspective and was beginning to feel like a human being again, she was finding Simon's presence to be as disturbing as ever.

"Want to talk about it?"

"Let's just say I overreacted. Haven't you ever let something or someone goad you until you lost control?" she asked in an attempt to divert the questions she knew were coming.

"No," Simon bluntly answered. "If I allowed that to happen, I'd be out of business. Exactly what did Stella Lang say to you that upset you so?" He favored her with an undivided attention that Adrian would have been just as happy to do without.

"How did you know it was Stella?"

"Sara, intelligent person that she is, told me that Jason's loving parent came flying out of your office as though jet propelled. Before Sara could get to you, you flew past her, hellbent on taking a nice, leisurely stroll in sixty-degree weather with a steady downpour as added inducement. What did that interfering old crone say to you?"

107

Adrian had to grin. She could just imagine Stella's reaction at being referred to as a crone, an old one at that. "I'd rather not talk about it, Simon," she murmured. "I made a stupid mistake and you rescued me. Can't we leave it at that?"

"If you were dealing with a warm, sensitive person, then yes," Simon pointed out with painful clarity. "But Stella has about as much sensitivity as a rattlesnake. Whatever she has on you, you can rest assured she'll make excellent use of it."

"She can't blackmail me, if that's what you're implying," Adrian informed him. "Even Jason knows the details of what Stella considers her ultimate weapon against me."

"Oh? Well, then, if Jason and Stella know, why not tell me?" he asked silkily. He sat forward long enough to remove a cigar from the lacquered box on the coffee table. After getting it going to his satisfaction, he looked at Adrian's bent head and the finely sculptured outline of her features. "Are you afraid to trust me with your secret?"

She looked up and met his gaze squarely. "No, I'm not afraid to trust you with a confidence. My secret, as you call it, happens to be something I've never wanted to shout from the rooftop. Unfortunately, Stella might do just that."

"Tell me about it. Perhaps I can do something to stop her."

Adrian stared at him, seeing character and strength underlying the harshness of his features. She'd sampled his anger, his passion, and his kindness. He may be devious as sin in other aspects of his

108

life, and she knew for certain he was manipulating Jason, but she would have to tackle that problem another time. This was here and now, and she needed to pull from that enormous strength and vitality that emanated from his forceful presence.

"I honestly think that at this moment I'd like to say that I have some sort of glamorous, exciting past . . . perhaps the mistress of some wealthy man. But" —she shrugged her slim shoulders—"I can't. I suppose one could say my life has been quiet. But looking back, I suppose it's been of my own choosing. At any rate, I'm reasonably happy, my business is doing well, and I have Jason, much to his mother's despair."

"But now she thinks she has a weapon against you, correct?"

"Yes. She waltzed into my office today, as pleased as punch with herself. She or someone she hired to do her dirty work for her did some checking on me and found out that I'm illegitimate." She waited for some sign from Simon, some betraying gesture. When it didn't come, she went on. "I listened to her insults and then I told her that Jason had known about my birth since we became engaged. That really set her off. I held on till she left and then I had to get out of there."

"Shame on you, Adrian, for letting that witch drive you to such lengths," came Simon's husky reproval. "At least you didn't let her know how bad she hurt you."

"Gee, thanks," she said sarcastically. "At least I did something right. I suppose you could have come through the entire confrontation without a second thought," she flared at him.

"Probably," Simon announced without the slightest hesitation. "But that's what makes us individuals. Personally, my dear Miss Kohl, I don't give a tinker's damn how you came into this world; I'm only delighted that you did."

His warm gaze held her angry blue one until he saw a softening in the velvet depths and a smile hovering about her lips.

"Has anyone ever told you that you're a bully?" Adrian eventually managed amid the curious sensations that were warming her from her head to the tips of her toes.

"Many times. But I make it a practice never to be swayed by other people's opinions. And in the future you do the same. For I'll be looking over your shoulder all the way," he predicted huskily.

"Are you threatening me, Mr. Lord?"

"Oh, yes, Miss Kohl. I'm threatening every single, delectable inch of you. I carry the picture of your lovely face with me wherever I go. I dream about you. I even plan devious methods by which to see you. You could say that you've taken top priority in my scheme of things." He reached over and ran his palm down one side of her face, letting it come to rest on the creamy softness of her neck. "Does that shock that prudish little soul of yours?" he rasped.

Adrian caught at his hand and stilled its disturbing touch. "I . . . you . . . Why do you say things like that?" she stammered.

"This is why." He leaned closer, the weight of his

110

much larger body pressing her deeper into the soft cushions. His lips brushed against her startled ones like warm velvet. That such tenderness could come from such a huge man amazed her.

All at once the feathery caresses weren't enough and his mouth became hard and insistent as it roamed over her own. Adrian was torn between desire and guilt. She struggled to remain impassive, but each second was like a time bomb nearing its moment of explosion. When it came, she opened her lips to him, laying bare her need and the rising passion that stormed within her.

She tasted the teasing tip of his tongue as it darted in its exciting torment. The taste and scent of him thrilled her, bringing her alive in ways she'd never felt before.

When one large hand slipped inside the robe and palmed the thrusting creaminess of her breast, a tiny groan of satisfaction rushed past Adrian's lips and was absorbed by Simon.

She felt the loosening of the robe as his warm hands ran from her breast to her hip, igniting tiny fires of desire in their path. She was spinning . . . spinning and she never wanted it to stop.

But it did stop and Adrian protested. When Simon would have pushed himself away from her, she tightened her arms about his neck, greedy for the continuation of this exquisite release he was meting out to her.

"You're not making this easy for me, you beautiful witch," he whispered against her ear. He caught her face between his hands and stared down at her.

There was a rosy glow in her cheeks and her eyes were dark and mysterious. "I want you, Adrian, but not now. You've been hurt and you're reaching out to somebody . . . anybody." He let one thumb softly caress the swollen moistness of her bottom lip and smiled. "I'm glad I was the one who found you. I'd hate to think of your responding to another man this way."

Adrian fought against the hard, cold reality that was slowly returning. She'd wanted Simon and she'd shown him how much. "I've made a fool of myself, haven't I?" she whispered.

"No, honey. You merely acted like a normal person. You responded openly and freely. What's so bad about that?"

"An engaged woman should only respond so openly and freely with her fiancé," Adrian muttered huskily.

Simon's face took on an expression that was frightening. "Your timing leaves a lot to be desired, Miss Kohl," he remarked icily. He never took his eyes off her as he pushed himself upright. He ran a hand through his dark hair, a heavy scowl masking his face. "I'll see if your clothes are dry. I'm sure you're dying to rush home and wait for Jason's call. Perhaps he'll be too busy with his blond companion to think about you. Has that disturbing thought occurred to you?"

"That's a rotten thing to say," Adrian flared. She clutched the front of the robe together and sat up. "You're hoping that will happen, aren't you, Simon? Why do you dislike him so?"

112

Simon coolly observed her, his mouth a rigid slash across the granite features. "I think what just happened between us should answer your question. If not, I'll be only too happy to fill in the gaps," he snarled.

"I get the picture," she muttered in a mutinous voice. "However, I still resent your sending Jason off with Janelle Kroft. I'm sure other arrangements could have been made for her."

"My dear Adrian," he shot back in a stinging voice. "I run my business for a profit, not to satisfy the whims of a redheaded, blue-eyed witch, regardless of how appealing I find her to be. As for your precious Jason, if he wasn't capable of carrying out the job I hired him to do, he wouldn't be in Denver now." He rose to his formidable height. "I'll check on your clothes."

Adrian watched him leave the room with an angry glimmer in her eyes. He'd made her sound foolish, as though asking him for special favors for Jason. Even though he denied it, she still believed he deliberately paired Jason and Janelle together.

While she waited she let her gaze wander around the spacious room. Apparently Simon used this as a combination den and office. The large desk in one corner certainly attested to such an assumption. Its top was strewn with papers and folders. The rest of the room, however, was warm and attractive. There was plenty of space—two large sofas and a number of chairs and small tables. Obviously her host didn't like to feel cramped.

When Simon reappeared with her clothes, Adrian

took them and went back to the bedroom she'd been in previously and changed.

Now that her thoughts were more settled, she looked about with interest. A king-size bed dominated the room, which bore the same hugeness as the den. A tall chest, two overstuffed chairs, and a table completed the furnishings. There were no pictures on the wall other than a large portrait of a woman which hung above the two chairs.

After slipping on her blazer, Adrian walked over and looked at the portrait. There was a sudden chill in her body as she stared at the lovely face of the young woman. The artist had caught a sense of devilment in her expression. It showed in her dark eyes and in the smile. Her long black hair was worn loose. It resembled a dark cloud resting on the woman's creamy shoulders.

"Lovely, isn't she?" came Simon's voice from the doorway.

Adrian whirled around, embarrassed at being caught staring, not to mention the fact that she hadn't heard him knock. "Do you usually creep up on people?" she asked cuttingly.

"Only when it's a beautiful young woman in my bedroom. I also happen to need a jacket," he threw over his shoulder as he walked over and opened the closet door.

"Do you like the portrait?"

"Yes. She's lovely," Adrian said softly. "You must care for her very much." She was dying to know who the woman was, but she was determined not to ask.

"Oh, I do . . . I do. We've had some good times together. Now that she's married though, I won't be able to see her as often," he calmly replied. He thrust his arms into the jacket, his dark eyes carefully watching Adrian.

"Oh."

"I'm hoping she'll visit me soon. When she does, I'd like for you to meet her."

"I—I'm sure you'll be busy once she arrives."

"Nonsense," Simon chuckled close behind her, his breath fanning her neck. "My sister goes at life non-stop. She'll come to care for you almost as much as I do." Two huge arms caught Adrian and pulled her back against a broad chest and hard, firm thighs. Simon's lips sought and found the smoothness of her neck beneath the fragrant fall of hair. "Were you jealous, Adrian?" he whispered.

She thought about disclaiming any such notion, then decided against it. He could read her far too well to swallow such a story. She shrugged. "A little. I was also shocked that you'd speak so casually about her. I had visions of your packing her husband off to Siberia with a stunning blonde while you went to bed with his wife," she honestly admitted.

The rumble of laughter that started deep in his chest brought a smile of chagrin to Adrian's face. Simon spun her about and clasped her to him in a tight embrace. When he could finally speak, he bent down and kissed the tip of her small nose.

"You are a delight. One minute I want to make love to you . . . the next finds me ready to strangle you and then you make me laugh." There was such

115

tenderness, such gentleness reflected in his face as he stared down at her, that Adrian wanted to cry. She raised a hand and touched her fingers to his face in an effort to stave off this peculiar sadness that was attacking her.

"I see so many questions in your eyes, sweetheart, so much hurt. I could make it all go away so easily. But," he sighed, "you're very stubborn. You insist on fighting me. So, we'll do it your way."

"You speak in riddles half the time," Adrian quietly admonished him. "I never know for sure what you're saying."

"You will, and soon." He looked over at the bed and his robe she'd neatly folded. "Are you ready?"

CHAPTER EIGHT

Instead of returning to the office Adrian decided to go home. The day was almost over, and she really wasn't in much of a mood to see anyone.

Simon insisted she give him the keys to her car. "I'll see that it's returned. You can also set your mind at ease about Stella Lang," he added. "I think once I have a few words with her she'll be happy to forget the whole matter."

"I really don't think you . . ."

"Shut up, Adrian," he ordered crossly. "I'll handle the matter and there'll be no repercussions, I promise."

Rather than argue further, which would be pointless, she gave in. And after thinking about it for a moment, she began to like the idea. She could almost see Stella agreeing to anything Simon suggested.

Before he let her out at her apartment, Simon

reached over and caught her hand in his huge grip. "You're not planning on going out this evening, are you?" His dark eyes pinned hers, holding her without exerting the slightest effort.

"No." Her voice came out husky. "I'll putter around the apartment for the rest of the afternoon, after I've called Sara, then have a TV dinner and get an early night." She smiled, thinking how ridiculous she sounded, reciting her proposed activities like an obedient child. "Does that meet with your approval?"

Simon lifted one shoulder, his bottom lip caught between strong white teeth. "Sounds lonely, but apparently that's the way you want it."

"Good-bye, Simon . . . and thanks," she murmured, then scurried from the car like a timid squirrel.

She refused to look back as she hurried toward the welcome façade of brick and mortar. She knew he was still there, sitting and watching. He was an enigma, and even though she'd seen another side of his personality, Adrian knew she was no closer to figuring out Simon Lord than when their relationship had consisted of only two voices on the telephone.

Sara was bursting with curiosity when Adrian finally called her.

"I've been frantic," she cried as soon as she recognized Adrian's voice. "I even considered calling the police, but I figured you'd kill me if I did."

"Correct," Adrian laughed. "I'm sorry, Sara, but Stella annoyed me so, I wasn't thinking clearly. I'm also sorry for dumping everything in your lap. Has it been very hectic?"

"So-so. I've managed to cope somewhat. By the way, Sandra called four times. I unthinkingly blurted out what had happened and she's really upset."

"Oh, dear. Well, look, let me call her and calm her down. Why don't you close early and go home. I promise to be at my desk in the morning at the crack of dawn."

"I'll hold you to that," Sara laughed. They ended the conversation on a laugh, then Adrian dialed the Cromiers' number.

"Where on earth have you been?" Sandra exclaimed. "Sara and I have been going out of our minds, Adrian. That was very inconsiderate of you," her friend accused.

"I know, Sandra, and I'm sorry. Things got a little out of hand, but I'm fine now. So you can stop worrying."

"Humph!" Sandra snorted. "You're not getting off that easy. I've just made a fresh pot of coffee. Why don't you come over and have a cup?"

"What you're really saying is come over and tell me what happened, isn't it?" Adrian laughed.

"Something like that," Sandra quipped, determined to stand her ground. "I suppose I could come over there," she began in a faintly accusing tone.

"Don't you dare come out in this weather," Adrian warned. "I'll be over there in a few minutes. I just want you to know though, that I'm perfectly aware of your scheming. If you weren't pregnant, I'd tell you to mind your own business."

"Oh, well, we win some, we lose some. I'll expect you in thirty minutes." The sharp click of a receiver being replaced and then the steady buzzing of the dial tone caused Adrian to shake her head in amusement.

"If allowed, Sandra would appoint herself guardian of the entire world," she murmured on her way to her bedroom.

She hurried to the closet and grabbed a pair of jeans and a blue sweater in a bulky knit. She quickly undressed and pulled on the jeans. Her head was buried in the thickness of the sweater when it hit her that she didn't have a car.

"Damn!" Her muttered oath sounded muffled. She pulled the sweater in place and rushed over to the telephone by her bed. She called for a taxi and was told one would be at her address in ten minutes.

"I hope Sandra appreciates the fact that I'll be exhausted by the time I get to her house," she groaned as she hurried into the bathroom to brush her hair and throw on some makeup. Regardless of the time, she thought as she studied her reflection, she wasn't blessed with a face that could greet the world without makeup.

"I hope you know that I'm a wreck now that I've been forced to rush so," Adrian remarked a short time later. She and Sandra were seated at the table in the cozy breakfast room, with Sandra determined to get to the bottom of her friend's weird flight from her office.

"Serves you right. I'm certain I got two gray hairs from worrying about you."

"They won't show. You blondes are lucky." Adrian eyed Sandra over the rim of her cup.

"What was Stella up to today?" Sandra asked.

Suddenly there was little humor left in Adrian at the mention of Stella's name. "She hoped to force me to break my engagement to Jason by threatening to expose my illegitimacy."

"She didn't!" Sandra exclaimed in profound shock. "Oh, honey, that's terrible," she wailed. "What are you going to do?"

"Calm down, Sandra," Adrian smiled gently. She reached across the table and patted her friend's hand. "Jason already knows. I told him all about it before I accepted his ring."

"You would handle it that way," Sandra murmured approvingly. "It's a darn shame his mother doesn't possess some of the same principles. Oh, Adrian. I'm so sorry this has happened. I've always admired the way you handled the situation." She grinned rather sheepishly. "In fact, after you first told me about it, and also threatened my life if I repeated the story, I was quiet envious."

"Envious? Of me?"

"I know, it's crazy," she chuckled. "But it made you more of a heroine to me. You were always so daring, always a leader. It gave you a certain mystique. I was bitterly disappointed that I couldn't claim such an auspicious beginning."

Adrian shook her head, amusement lurking in her eyes. "No wonder I was always having to get you out

121

of scrapes. With fantasies like that, you were dangerous. Auspicious beginning indeed! Let's hope your
child has his father's level head and straight thinking."

Before Sandra could defend herself, the back door
opened to reveal David.

"This is too much," he grinned in mock distress.
"I've slaved all day at the office. Now I find not one,
but two women to contend with."

"Consider yourself lucky, you ungrateful brute,
and close the door," his wife informed him.

Adrian laughed at this exchange between husband
and wife. There was a certain security in their love,
a oneness that shined through when they were
together. She'd often wondered what it would be like
to have such a relationship with a man.

"Would you have me be rude to our guest, Mrs.
Cromier?" David asked mysteriously.

"Our guest isn't in need of additional cold air or
dampness," Sandra sternly reminded him. "So close
the door and stop acting like a two-year-old."

"Madam, I resent that. David assured me that you
were always in the best of moods," Simon teased as
his large frame suddenly loomed behind David's.
"Now I hear you going at this poor man like a
fishwife." The smile he gave Sandra, however, was
conspiciously absent as he let his dark gaze touch on
Adrian.

"Simon!" Sandra exclaimed. "What a nice surprise." She rose to her feet. "Let me get two more
steaks from the freezer. I insist you and Adrian stay
for dinner."

122

"Thank you, but I'm afraid we can't," he answered without consulting Adrian. He walked toward her, halting when he was directly behind her. His hands dropped to her shoulders and began to gently knead the tense muscles. "This young lady is supposed to be relaxing and having an early night. I had no idea she planned on paying social calls to all her friends."

"You—you didn't? I mean . . ." Sandra helplessly floundered amid this new and exciting development. "Just why are you so concerned with how Adrian spends her afternoons?" she finally got out.

"Sandra, will you stop it?" David sighed. "You shouldn't ask such personal questions."

"Yes, Sandra, do as your husband tells you," Adrian chimed in. She knew Sandra was about to explode from wanting to know what was going on, and Adrian was amused by her frustrations.

"You're all being mean, but I suppose I'll survive. Do you have time for a cup of coffee?" She directed the question toward Simon.

"Yes, please." He relinquished his hold on Adrian, but only long enough to pull a chair close to her and sit down. Even then, one long arm found its way across her shoulders, causing a tiny shiver of delight to race through her veins.

At the same time, she felt strange in allowing him this liberty. Sandra and David were Jason's friends as well, although at times Adrian wasn't so sure whether they really liked him or merely accepted him for her sake.

This definitely wasn't the case with Simon. For in

123

spite of the questions ready to tumble from her lips at the slightest provocation, Sandra seemed enormously pleased.

While she was getting the additional cups, having enlisted David's help as well, Simon took advantage of the opportunity to let Adrian know he was less than pleased that she hadn't done as she'd promised.

"I can see now that taking care of yourself is the least of your worries," he growled in her ear. The hand that cupped the pivotal point of her shoulder tightened. "That annoys me, Miss Kohl."

"Really, Mr. Lord?" she retorted in a sugary voice guaranteed to irritate him. She turned and faced him. "Then I'm afraid you'll have to get in line. Between you, Sara, and Sandra, I feel as though I've been thoroughly grilled." She'd meant to put him in his place with her cute remarks, but his close proximity, his face only inches from her own, was causing her pulse to beat in a most erratic manner.

"If you keep looking at me that way, I'm going to kiss you," he murmured. His threat caused Adrian to inch back in her chair, an embarrassing pink rushing to her cheeks. "You do that so nicely, Adrian. Blushing is a dying art," he chuckled.

"Not with you around," she remarked dryly. "How did you know I was here?"

"David. He was at my office. Before he left, he called Sandra. She told him that you were on your way over to have coffee with her. I overheard the conversation and decided that you were playing hooky. That's when I took matters into my own hands and told David a little of what had happened."

124

Simon smiled somewhat ruefully. "He must have sensed something in my voice, because he invited me to stop by and have a drink. I'd have come after you anyway, invitation or not. You know that, don't you?"

Adrian dropped her gaze, not wanting to accept what she saw in his eyes, closing her ears to the certainty in his voice.

"I'm glad you have the Cromiers for friends," Simon said later as he and Adrian were driving back to her apartment. "Does David know the whole story?"

"Of course. Sandra never keeps anything from him. Though she did ask me first if she could tell him." Her voice was cold and remote. She was still rattled from the open possessivness he'd shown. It was as though he held some great secret regarding her future in his hands and was simply playing a game with her, gaining immense pleasure from watching her stumble and falter like a mouse in a maze before swooping down and rescuing her.

His plan of attack had been swift and sure. He had steadily encroached upon her thoughts and her mind. Even her dreams had become a battleground. She found him to be sensual and desirable, neither emotion bringing with it a soothing force.

When the car eased to the curb in front of her apartment, Adrian turned to Simon for the second time that day, a precise little speech of thanks ready to tumble from her lips. Before she could say a word, he switched off the motor, withdrew the key, and got out of the car.

She watched him walk around the front of the car to the passenger side. When he opened her door and extended his hand, she hesitated only briefly before allowing hers to be swallowed in his warm grasp.

"You don't have to see me to the door," she told him, her eyes focusing somewhere in the region of his chest.

"Oh . . . I think so," Simon casually remarked. "Besides, I'm hungry. I plan on raiding your fridge."

"But—but . . ."

"Tsk, tsk. You should have that stammer checked, Adrian," he suggested solicitously. "You've been doing that quite a lot lately."

"There's nothing wrong with my speech, Simon Lord, and you damn well know it. It's you that's causing me problems," she cried as she hurried to keep up with his giant strides. "Slow down, you big idiot," she ordered him. It was humiliating trying to get her point across when she was forced to scamper along like an excited chicken!

Simon looked down at her from his considerable height, a cheeky grin on his face. "Why on earth should I slow down? That would give you more time to fuss. You seem determined to start a fight with me, and I don't want that to happen."

"Ha!" Adrian scornfully muttered. "Don't flatter yourself. All I want is for you to get back into your car and drive out of my life. Is that so difficult to understand?"

By then they were at the door and she was scrambling in her purse for her key. "Ever since I met you, you've done nothing but criticize me, my life, and my fiancé." She jammed the key in the lock and flung open the door, then turned and glared at Simon. "Will you please be a gentleman—probably for the first time in your life—and go?"

In an unexpected move Simon reached out and caught her by her upper arms and quite easily moved her aside. He came into the room, slamming the door shut with his foot. "No." He uttered the one word pleasantly enough and waited, arms folded across his chest, for the explosion.

But Adrian was speechless. She'd never before met such an immovable object. She'd insulted him, screamed at him, and he still wouldn't listen.

She heaved a huge sigh of frustration, stalked over to the sofa, and dropped her purse. "Are you really hungry?" She eyed him suspiciously over her shoulder.

"Famished. I'm particularly partial to omelets," he told her in a voice that was soft and seductive.

"You'll take pot luck and be happy," she snapped on her way to the kitchen.

The only sound that could be heard for the next few minutes was the banging of cupboard doors and the thumping of pots and pans.

When the first haunting notes of her newest Henry Mancini album sounded, Adrian became still. One hand was firmly gripping the edge of a mixing bowl, the other holding a wooden spoon. A pleasant expression of surprise softened her face. Perhaps music was a good idea, she thought. It usually drew her out of her depressed state and lifted her spirits.

Suddenly she froze. "Good Lord! Is he deaf?" For instead of beautiful and melodious, it sounded as though ten thousand sets of drums, trumpets, and guitars had chosen her living room as a concert hall. In a flash Adrian dropped the spoon into the bowl and dashed to the door and flung it open. "Turn that down!" she yelled to Simon, who was leaning with one elbow against the wall directly above the stereo, his other hand on his hip.

When he didn't immediately obey her, she rushed over and grasped the knob, stopping the deafening sound.

"What on earth are you trying to do, get me evicted?" she yelled at him. His implacable expression hadn't changed since she rushed into the room.

"You mean you didn't appreciate all the noise?" he innocently asked.

"Of course not," she snapped in tight-lipped disapproval.

"That's odd. From the way you were slamming things around in the kitchen, I thought you would approve."

There was a pregnant silence as they stared at each other. Adrian was forced to admit a grudging admiration for the man. She'd ignored him and he'd retaliated. Finally she began to find the entire incident funny.

Seeing the softening of her features and the sparkle in her eyes, Simon said, "Truce?" and held out his hand.

She honestly couldn't call it indifference or weariness from a long, disturbing day that made her extend her own hand. It was more like she was willed to form a pact with Simon, a pact that would protect them against the world, and one that held untold pleasures for her if she would only accept them.

"Truce," Adrian whispered. She withdrew her hand and started back to the kitchen. The expression in Simon's eyes was disturbing, forcing her into a position she wasn't finding at all comfortable.

Instead of staying put in the living room as she hoped he would, Simon followed her into the tiny compact kitchen. "May I ask what that is?" He was standing beside her and was looking at the mixture in the bowl with the most dubious of expressions.

"Quiche," she informed him with a smothered grin. "There's tuna and fresh mushrooms, along with the usual eggs, cheese, and cream. It's very nutritious."

"If you say so. Are you a health-food addict?"

An irrepressible giggle escaped Adrian. "Don't worry, Simon. I'm not about to offer you alfafa sprouts. Does that satisfy you?" she asked as she poured the mixture into the waiting pie shell.

"It certainly does. My sister eats the damnedest stuff you've ever seen, and she's always trying to force it on me. For a minute there I was afraid you had the same tastes in food," he told her in a relieved voice.

"Well, you can rest at ease." She put the quiche into the oven and closed the door. She turned, her eyes running appraisingly over the seemingly endless length of her guest. "When you plan on dining with a person, Simon, you should give them advance warning. Trying to prepare enough food to fill you up isn't easy." She turned and opened a cupboard and began looking over her supply of canned vegetables. "How are you at making a salad?"

"The best," he answered unhesitatingly.

"You would be," Adrian muttered sarcastically to herself. "The makings are in the fridge."

"Do I detect a note of sarcasm?" he chuckled, having heard her plainly enough.

"No, merely resignation."

"Then we're making progress." He sounded pleased. "Perhaps in the future you'll stop questioning my every move."

"That isn't likely to happen, and you know it. Questions and arguments are my only defense against you."

"You're still annoyed with me because of Janelle, aren't you?"

"Yes, yes, I am." Adrian busied herself with opening a can of baby peas, refusing to look up. "You deliberately threw her at Jason, hoping he'd take the bait. I'll be glad when he returns so that I can say I told you so."

Simon paused in his salad-making and regarded her through shuttered lids. "You really think that's what will happen?"

"Certainly." She sounded far more confident than she felt. She wasn't at all sure about Jason, but she could never reveal that to Simon. It would be too great a weapon.

"Is that why you went to such lengths at dinner the other night to let Janelle and me know that you planned to rush straight home and hop into bed . . . with Jason? Were you hoping to warn her off?" he jeered.

"Something like that. Didn't you appreciate my performance?" Her voice was cool and flat. "I think it was excellent."

"Oh, it was, Adrian, it really was. Janelle swallowed the whole bit. But I know you, and I also know Jason. Your feelings for him are such that going to bed with him is the furthest thing from your mind. As for Jason, he stands almost in greater awe of you than he does his mother. He's dominated by both you and Stella."

For once Adrian didn't have a ready comeback. She kept her attention fixed on preparing the meal, but her thoughts were reeling from Simon's remarks.

In past moments of retrospect she, too, had been forced to admit that Jason was a bone of contention between her and Stella. Neither of them was willing to give an inch. It had become a battle of wills, with Jason being the prize to the victor.

CHAPTER NINE

True to her promise to Sara, Adrian was at her desk by seven thirty the next morning. Contrary to her fears that tossing and turning would be her reward, she went to sleep without the least effort.

"Maybe Simon does have his uses after all," she murmured with a rueful twist of her mouth as she got to her feet and walked over to the coffeepot that had just that moment stopped its rhythmic perking.

She let her thoughts fade back over the evening spent with Simon. Somehow he always managed to evoke a gamut of emotions within her. Anger, amusement, and sometimes sadness. But she'd found that after each encounter with him she felt invigorated, and last night was no exception.

Admit it, she chided herself. *He has forced you out of the safe, uneventful rut your life was in. Granted, the transition could prove painful, but you're more alive than you ever dreamed possible.*

Adrian knew it had been compassion that made him brave her temper the night before. He'd said as much as they relaxed on the sofa and listened to the music. There was only the soft glow from one lamp lighting the room. It was cozy and Adrian was as content as a purring kitten.

"Are you certain you aren't still upset from what Stella Lang did?" Simon asked. Her head was resting on his shoulder, and his arm was holding her close. She hadn't exactly figured out how they'd come to be in such a position, and frankly she didn't care. She was finding that being cuddled by Simon was very agreeable.

"Thanks to you, I haven't thought about it at all since we left Sandra's," she confessed somewhat sheepishly. "I've been so busy fighting with you, there's been no time left for anything else."

"Are you pleased about that?" he smiled down at her. "Or are you going to find fault with my methods for treating shock."

Adrian found herself being drawn into the dark, compelling depths of his eyes, and nothing on earth could save her. "No . . . I can't find any fault," she sighed.

"You're beautiful, Adrian, do you know that?" He bent his head and whispered against her lips. "Beautiful and so desirable." The tip of his tongue teased her bottom lip, the touch causing her heart to race wildly.

He soon tired of that pleasurable dalliance and

pulled her across his lap. His lips became seductive, commanding as the kiss deepened, and he took charge of her softly yielding mouth.

Of their own volition she felt her arms slowly inching upward to broad shoulders. Her fingers were soon lost in the dark hair that softly brushed his nape.

Their breathing was ragged, reduced to short gasps which, mingled with the soft mews of pleasure, vied with the haunting music in the background.

With passion urging her on, giving her a certain reckless courage, Adrian found herself wanting more than kisses that left her aching for release. Her hands moved downward, her fingers gliding over cashmere-clad muscle and warmth till they reached the waistband of Simon's dark trousers.

Uncaring of the consequences, intent only in assuaging the gnawing craving inside her, she ran her hands beneath the sweater. Simon became still as her fingers began to slowly, haltingly, explore a man's torso for the first time.

There was excitement quickening her senses as she touched his rib cage, his taut midriff, finding even greater delight in the crisp growth that covered his chest. She was like a sightless person, the sensitive tips of her fingers committing to memory every inch of his tanned chest. . . .

"Why don't you open your eyes and look at me?" Simon's voice caressed her. "Don't be shy," he whispered.

Adrian did look at him then, at her fingers, pale against the bronze of his skin. When he caught the sweater and pulled it over his head, she continued to stare, one part of her marveling at how little embarrassment she felt at openly admiring this man's body, the other part wanting to feel that same body against hers.

As though reading her thoughts, Simon reached for the edges of her sweater and slipped it up and over her head, leaving only the modest covering of her bra to conceal her breasts from his gaze. The front clasp gave under his practiced hand, the piece of wispy lace fluttering to the floor forgotten.

The contact of a slightly abrasive palm cupping the gentle weight of first one breast and then the other sent a tremor throughout Adrian's body. Her nails dug into Simon's shoulders as his lips followed his hands, his tongue nudging her rigid nipples with a slow, deliberate motion that was maddening.

She'd never dreamed that a man's hand against her waist, her shoulder, gliding down her back, could set her on fire, leaving her body shamelessly arching for fulfillment.

"Adrian." Simon gasped her name in a voice grown thick with passion. "I'm going to make love to you." He was leaning over her, his upper body supported by his elbows. "Do you understand me?" he whispered, one hand unable to leave the proud thrust of her breasts, their rosebud tips beckoning him to taste their sweetness.

"Yes, I understand. I want that too." She met his gaze without flinching.

"Are you sure?"

"Yes."

There was a curious brilliance in his eyes as he stared down at her, triumphant but tempered with something Adrian couldn't quite put her finger on.

In one single move he stood up, then reached down for her and swung her high in his arms. His mouth took hers again, his tongue plunging into her softness and bringing a response from her that had her clutching at his shoulders, her senses reeling.

Simon carried her to the bedroom and stood her on her feet beside the bed. Without speaking, he knelt before her, his hands busy with the heavy snap and zipper of her jeans. With movements ever so gentle he removed the garment and then slowly slipped his fingers beneath the last fragile barrier. He drew the satin bikini down over her thighs until every inch of her was bared to him in the semi-darkness of the room.

"You're like a statue that's been lovingly and painstakingly formed. Tonight I'm going to breathe life into you. You're going to come alive in such a way, your body will never forget me," he whispered hoarsely.

He touched his lips to her thighs, his tongue forging a flaming trail upward over her stomach, her waist, her midriff. Her breasts were worshipped and finally he took her waiting lips. Adrian clutched him to her, her body burning, pressing against his as she communicated her need to him.

Without completely withdrawing from her, Simon dealt with the remainder of his clothes, and his massive body trembled when he felt Adrian's hands learning the newness of him. There was an indrawn gasp of surprise from her as her fingers lightly probed at the taut flatness of his stomach and the hardness of his thighs.

Deftly and with an ease of motion she'd come to expect from him, Simon lifted her in his arms and stepped to the bed, their combined weights making a single indentation in the blue coverlet.

Adrian felt firm thighs easing between hers—felt a tingling sensation as the tips of her breasts meshed with the roughness of the hair on his chest. She opened her arms to him, her body and her soul.

"Hang on, my darling," he whispered against her ear. "This is for real. There'll be no pulling back now." And there wasn't.

He held and guided her each exploding step of the way, and she clung to him and blindly followed. They touched the heights of ecstasy at the same moment, then rode the waves of numbness till light and sound and thought again penetrated the aura of their passion.

There weren't enough words in Adrian's vocabulary to adequately describe the overwhelming fulfillment that reached out and settled over every inch of her body.

She was snuggled close to Simon's wide chest, his arms wrapped around her like twin hawsers of steel. At some point during or after they'd made love he had managed to pull the sheet over them. Beneath it Adrian was aware, disturbingly so, of the muscular hardness of one strong thigh thrust between her own slim ones, of their naked bodies snug and relaxed against each other.

Simon's breathing was easy and unlabored. Adrian wondered if he was sleeping or pretending. But that's silly, she told herself. She knew he'd shared this same moment with any number of women before, and probably would again, she sighed resignedly. Those thoughts weren't pleasant, but there was no point in kidding herself. Simon was like a wily fox, and no one woman could hope to hold him for longer than he cared to let her.

She considered the wisdom of the last few hours. Unfortunately the incident couldn't be wiped away as easily as erasing a blackboard. Neither could Simon be dismissed in such a manner.

From the beginning, his pursuit of her had been relentless. Now with Jason working for Lord Electronics, Adrian knew future meetings with Simon would be inevitable, and she wasn't at all certain how she was going to handle seeing him.

"That was a very wistful sigh, Adrian," he murmured in a gravelly voice close to her ear. "Don't tell me you're tiring of me already." There was a hypnotic pull in the slow, easy sweep of his large hand as it caressed the smoothness of her hip.

He eased her onto her back, then raised himself on one elbow and stared down at her. "I know I made you happy, made you forget everything, and you sure as hell pleased me."

Adrian was unable to control the smile that caught at her lips. "Are you asking me or telling me that I enjoyed having you make love to me?" she teased.

There wasn't enough light to really see his face, but she didn't have to. She raised her hand and let her fingers gently trace the wide forehead and the prominent bone beneath his brows. His nose, its beaklike shape, gave way to lips that had intrigued her from the beginning. And even in darkness there could be no mistaking his stubborn chin and unyielding jaw.

A poignant silence hovered over them, bringing to Adrian an awareness of an inexplicable feeling for this man that left her momentarily shaken. Pulling on a strength she didn't know she possessed, she willed the catch at her heart, the sensation of suddenly plummeting from an unbelievable height to be still. Simon wasn't the sort of man a woman built dreams around.

"Now it's my turn to be the interrogator," she whispered, her voice husky. "You've become very silent all of a sudden."

Simon caught the hand that was still against his face and turned the palm to his lips. "I want you to move in with me, Adrian."

At first she thought she hadn't heard him correctly. But in the ensuing seconds that ticked by she knew there had been no mistake. She tried, unsuccessfully, to pull away from the insidious warmth of his body. "Why on earth should I even consider such a thing?" She tried for a light, indifferent pose, but in reality her tone of voice sounded forced and uncertain.

An impatient breath burst through Simon's lips and she could feel the tensing of the arm that was tight across her waist.

"Because, you stubborn little minx, we belong together. And don't insult me by waving your engagement ring under my nose," he callously reminded her, "for any doubts I might have had on that score are now quite cleared up."

"Oh? Then perhaps you'll explain your sudden mystical powers to me," she replied tartly. How dare he assume that she'd be willing to disrupt her life, not to mention Jason's, merely to provide him with a live-in mistress!

"It's quite simple, Adrian. Would you be here if your love for Jason was all it's cracked up to be?" he taunted. "If you were my fiancée, you can be damned sure I wouldn't have tolerated a year-long engagement. Nor would I have waited that long without making love to you."

"I should consider myself lucky then, shouldn't I, that it's Jason I'm engaged to and not you," she retorted. "You're such an insensitive brute, you haven't the remotest idea of what it means to respect one's wishes not to rush headlong into a relationship as serious as marriage."

"Bull!"

"I beg your pardon?"

"You heard me," Simon yelled. "Don't let it shock you. You'll hear far worse before we're through. I think it explains exactly to a T my opinion of your academy-award performance for stalling. Hell!" he scoffed derisively. "If you had any sense at all, you'd realize that anyone who's as patient as your loving Jason is has to be having some of the same doubts that've been plaguing you."

140

"Thank you, Mr. Lord! The field of psychiatry was denied a veritable genius when you chose the world of high finance."

This time she refused to be subdued by his confining arm. She jackknifed into a sitting position and glared at him. "I do not have doubts about Jason, thank you. And even if I did, listening to you would have made me realize what a kind, patient man he is. He has charm, a . . . a certain sensitivity that precludes the need to grab me and throw me into his bed like some ancient feudal lord."

There were tears in her eyes as she hurled the hateful insults at the huge, intimidating man. Damn him! He'd given her a brief glimpse of paradise and then snatched it from her grasp, leaving her hurt and disillusioned.

"Is that really what you think I've done, Adrian?" he softly asked. "That I forced myself on you?"

"No, you know I wasn't referring to . . . to us, here at this moment. I knew what was going on and I could have stopped you."

"Will you break off your engagement to Jason and move in with me?" His question was direct, his voice like cold steel.

"I can't, Simon."

There was the rustle of bedclothes as he pushed himself back till he was resting against the headboard of the bed. "So, we're to forget tonight and pretend a polite friendliness when we meet. Is that what you want?" he asked silkily.

"Why not? I'm sure we're not the first two people to lose control."

She felt more than saw him reach for her, but for the life of her she couldn't move. Before she could gather her scattered wits about her, Adrian found herself flat on her back, with Simon's body pushing her deeper into the mattress.

Her fingers were splayed ineffectually against his broad chest, his face only a hairbreadth above her own. She hated the traitorous pounding of her heart that sounded like a drum in her ears.

With a deliberateness that proved louder than words his mastery over her, Simon caught both her wrists in one large hand and eased them above her head where he held them. His other hand cupped the fullness of one breast while his tongue teased the throbbing tip until Adrian had to bite her lips to keep from crying out against the pleasure surging through her.

"Please, Simon," she whispered, "this isn't the way to solve anything." She turned her head from side to side as his hand worked its way, inch by inch, over her body, squeezing, caressing till she was writhing beneath him.

"The hell it isn't," he murmured huskily between greedy forays of his hot, moist lips upon the aroused warmth of her skin. "This is the only way I can reason with you, and believe me, I don't mind at all."

Adrian stopped protesting after that and became the willing student, with Simon the master in the blending of their bodies as one.

There was an unconscious drooping of the shoulders of the slim figure standing by her office window, her gaze locked into a trancelike state of concentration. The cup of coffee in her hand had long since ceased sending up its undulating trail of steam.

Her period of reflection had been long and disturbing, as were most of her thoughts regarding Simon. Adrian had always believed she was a strong individual. To suddenly find herself as pliable as a blade of grass in a storm was upsetting. Especially when the storm was Simon Lord.

Now that he'd broken down her defenses, Adrian knew he would intensify his attack. She had unwittingly presented him with a challenge, and Simon wouldn't let it rest until he got what he wanted. And heaven only knows what that is, she sighed wistfully.

Perhaps now that he'd added her to his list of conquests, he'd lose interest. Curiously enough, that fleeting thought didn't bring the comfort Adrian thought it would. A world without Simon would be a lonely place.

CHAPTER TEN

The respite Adrian hoped Simon would grant her after having spent the night at her apartment failed to materialize. Instead, it got to a point where she was afraid to turn a corner or open a door for fear of running into him. He was everywhere, and his dark gaze was relentless as he silently mocked her.

With Jason away so much of the time, Simon was indeed pressed into service as her escort. Not that Adrian asked him; she would have died first. But Sandra saw fit to have some friends over on two occasions, as did another couple Adrian knew.

Sandra took matters into her own hands by inviting Simon and asking him to bring Adrian. Seeing them together so frequently, others in the same group naturally assumed there was some sort of relationship between Adrian and Simon, and began to invite them as a couple.

During the spree of parties that seemed to be occurring with surprising regularity, Adrian decided to put her foot down. She firmly refused one particular invitation, determined to show Simon that she was on to his game and that she wouldn't be available for future dates with him.

On the night of the planned event, however, her doorbell sounded precisely at seven thirty. Adrian transferred some work she was going over to the table in front of the sofa and got to her feet.

She'd had her bath and was comfortably dressed in a blue flannel nightgown, its voluminous folds primly hiding every curve of her body. Nevertheless, she thought it prudent to peek through the peephole before flinging open the door.

A frown settled over her features as she caught sight of Simon's head and shoulders outside her door. She knew exactly why he was there and it angered her.

I'll not answer, she thought with a malicious twist of humor. *I'll get back to my work and Mr. Lord can go to the devil!*

She did just that, smiling widely at how cleanly she'd outsmarted Simon.

"He is insistent," Adrian softly murmured some minutes later after having endured the steady pealing of the doorbell, joined at intervals by a heavy-handed pounding on the door.

She sat through it all, showing only mild annoyance at the noise, and congratulated herself on a job well done, when eventually all was quiet.

Now that he'd come and gone, Adrian walked

over and turned on the television. There was a program she wanted to watch. She padded back to the sofa and sat down, then reached for the stack of folders she'd abandoned earlier.

Just as she leaned back she heard the distinct sound of a key being inserted into the lock. Before she could do more than stare transfixed, the door was thrust open and Simon catapulted into her living room like a well-trained commando. Hovering in the hallway, she saw Mr. Gately, the shy but nice manager of the building.

There was shock on all three faces as both men stared at Adrian and she at them. "Will someone please explain why my apartment has been broken into?" she asked icily. She stood, her outrage striking out at each astonished man like the flick of a whip. "Mr. Gately? Do you make a habit of passing out your tenants' keys to anyone who asks for them?"

"Er . . . no, Miss Kohl. That is . . ."

"Miss Kohl is overreacting, Mr. Gately, and rightly so. I'm afraid we frightened her," Simon soothed the extremely nervous little man. "Once I explain, she'll understand. Thanks for your help."

Mr. Gately, grateful to be escaping Adrian's obvious anger, cast her a last anxious look, then scampered away like a timid mouse.

Simon caught the edge of the door with one hand and slammed it shut, the noise ricocheting throughout the room like a gunshot. He faced Adrian, his suit jacket pushed back from his hips by his hands, his thumbs tucked in the waistband of his trousers. There was a curious gleam in his eyes as they slowly

146

took in the casualness of her dress and the well-scrubbed look of her shiny face. He then looked down at his own impeccably tailored dark suit, white shirt, and precisely correct tie.

"I wasn't aware that we were going to a costume party, Miss Kohl."

"I wasn't aware *we* were going anywhere, Mr. Lord," she told him in an angry rush. "I distinctly remember declining the Delrays' invitation."

With resigned forebearance Simon flicked back a snowy cuff and glanced at his watch. "It's only eight o'clock. We still have time. Unless"—he stared pointedly at her flannel gown—"you plan on going as you are."

"I'm not leaving my apartment this evening, Simon. I have work to do. So . . ." She allowed her voice to trail off. Surely he wasn't that dense.

There was a perceptible tightening of his lips. He calmly removed his jacket and carefully draped it over a chair, loosening his tie as he walked over and dropped down on the sofa. "Okay, let's have it. You're obviously upset about something. Once you get it off your chest you'll feel better."

"Off your duff and on your feet, Simon. I want you out of here right now," she ordered furiously. How dare he burst into her apartment, then attempt to act like her father confessor. She despised him and wanted him gone.

"Did you hear me?" She glared down at him, her fists resting on her hips in her most intimidating stance.

"How could I not?" he asked. "You're practically

147

standing over me and yelling at the top of your voice. Although I'm several years older than you, I don't suffer from a hearing problem."

Adrian fairly danced with frustration at this large hunk of humanity that had taken root on her very own sofa. "Damn you, Simon!" She really did yell at that point. "I refuse to tolerate another minute of your detestable presence. "Get . . . out," she very carefully enunciated the last words.

In a flash her wrist was seized and given a short, quick jerk. Before she could brace herself against this attack, Adrian felt herself falling. She landed in an ungainly heap of flannel, sprawled helplessly across Simon's broad thighs.

"Let me go," she spluttered in embarrassed outrage. Her plans for the evening weren't going at all as planned!

"No," he smiled dangerously, his mouth achingly close to her own. "I prefer staying in for a change. It's much nicer having you all to myself."

"You don't have me all to yourself, Simon, and I resent the implication," she retorted stiffly, refusing to look at the knowing gleam in his eyes.

"Ahh," he murmured. "Now I'm beginning to get the picture."

"Oh? Then perhaps you'll enlighten me."

"Of course, sweetheart," he agreed in a soothing tone as one hand released her long enough to reach up and remove the single clip that held her hair in casual disarray on top of her head. Once he'd laced his fingers through the auburn strands to his satisfaction, he shifted their positions so that her head was resting comfortably against his shoulder.

"Now . . . to answer your question," he began. "You're suddenly eaten up with guilt because we've been seeing each other and you've enjoyed it. You're more alive with me than you've ever been and you resent it. Plus"—he caught her left hand and held it, his fingers twisting her engagement ring—"this ridiculous charade you insist on continuing."

"My God!" she burst out. "You're ego is incredible. For your information, Jason and I have been quite close these past few weeks, in spite of your seeing that he doesn't get more than a day or two at home."

"Close enough to set a date?"

"That's none of your business." She evaded the question and wished she could do the same thing with his hand that was softly caressing her hip and thigh. "Stop it, Simon." She caught his hand and stopped the movement that was slowly turning her into a trembling mass.

"Are you telling or asking?" he softly asked.

Adrian let the tip of her pink tongue nervously dart over lips that were dry. "Please," she whispered. "You know I can't handle the pressure right now," and she wasn't kidding.

With Jason popping in for incredibly short periods of time, his every word devoted to regaling Adrian with the challenge of his new position, and Simon stalking her like a large, satisfied cat, she was fast becoming a basket case.

There was also something different about Jason.

He was attentive enough, but Adrian sensed a coolness toward her and she knew for a fact that he'd had a flaming row with his mother. There'd been no further mention of setting a date for their wedding. And it was his silence on this last item that nagged at her peace of mind.

Suddenly there was a sharp tug on the strand of her hair that had curled itself around Simon's finger.

"Ouch!" she cried. "That hurt me." She gave him an ugly look, her hand rubbing at her scalp.

"But it got your attention, didn't it?" His expression was implacable. "I'm not accustomed to holding a woman in my arms while she daydreams about another man."

"Tsk, tsk." Adrian couldn't help but grin at the petulant tone of his voice. "You can rest assured, Simon. My thoughts weren't entirely one-sided. You were most definitely included."

After that unsuccessful attempt to thwart Simon, Adrian wasn't so eager to try again. He wasn't as easily managed as Jason, and deep in her heart she knew she was pleased.

One Saturday morning, after declaring her apartment a disaster area, Adrian vowed not to step a foot outside her door until it was sparkling clean.

Her outfit for a morning of scrubbing and cleaning included a pair of faded denims left over from her late teen years. And while her body had gone from coltish litheness to willowy slimness, the denims had simply shrunk from repeated washings and now fit like the perverbial second skin.

Her sweat shirt, one of David's that she'd "borrowed" after having worn it while spending a weekend with him and Sandra, wasn't much better, except that where the denims were skin tight, two people could easily have gotten into the fullness of her favorite shirt.

As she worked she thought back to that evening's folly, when she'd thought she'd outsmart Simon. All she'd gotten for her stealth and cunning had been the certain knowledge that Simon was an expert when it came to reducing her to a quivering mass that only he could satisfy. The problem was, she remembered to her profound embarrassment, he'd called a halt to their lovemaking, leaving Adrian adrift, her nerves stretched to the breaking point.

"And you, my dense one, can hardly wait to be with him again," she murmured to herself as she renewed her efforts to reduce her small bathroom to a sparkling gem of cleanliness.

All during the time it took her to finish the bath and later, the bedroom, Adrian kept lecturing herself against the pitfalls of falling for Simon Lord. She mentally enumerated each fault, each failing of his and was smugly pleased at the mounting list.

"So why, knowing what I do, am I watching the clock like some impressionable teenager for my date with him this evening?" she asked derisively. She stared at her face in the mirror over the dressing table and scowled. "You, Adrian Kohl, are a simple-minded fool."

No amount of mental flagellation could erase from her mind the feel of Simon's hands on her body and the demanding kisses that always left her breathless and clinging.

And even though Simon hadn't made love to her again, Adrian knew he was only biding his time. There'd been more than that one occasion when he'd drawn the line at how far they went.

Away from him, she would spend hours plotting revenge, thinking up ways to extricate herself from his clutches, only to see her well-ordered plans flying out the window when his sensuous mouth took lazy possession of hers, when their eyes would meet at a party and that indefinable message would race between their locked gazes, ushering them into a time and place of oneness, oblivious to the sight and sound of the world about them.

"Oh, hell!" she muttered disgustedly, then turned from the betraying picture of herself and went on her way. So what if she loved the unscrupulous rake? For she did; of that she was certain. Surely it would pass. It had to. On the other hand, she thought realistically, there were few cases of people expiring from unrequited love!

Adrian was dressed and waiting well before the appointed time. She stood in the center of the bedroom, turning first one way and then the other in an attempt to see all sides of the dress she was wearing. She'd decided at least five times that it was perfect, only to be swamped moments later by waves of undermining doubt. It was this latter state of mind she was in at the moment, and indecision was causing her fingers to pick nervously at the jade green skirt and pull uneasily at the shiny, silver top with the thin spaghetti straps.

The outfit was stunning, but for once in her confident life, Adrian was a bundle of nerves. She moved and a considerable amount of nylon-clad leg peeked seductively from the long slit up the side of the skirt.

"Oh, no," she wailed. "This will never do. Simon will think I've dressed especially to please him." That she'd done precisely that very thing was beyond her realm of conscious thought. Only the two short jabs of the doorbell kept her from changing into something else.

With a tremulous quiver of her lips adding to the expression of vulnerability on her face, Adrian quickly left the bedroom and went to answer the door.

There was an alert narrowing of Simon's gaze as he stared at the vision of loveliness standing before him. Beneath the outer trappings of dress and the fixed, polite smile of greeting, he sensed panic.

He walked into the room and closed the door behind him. "You're beautiful, princess. And I especially like your dress." His voice caressed her, spreading over Adrian like a warm blanket of security.

"Do you really?" She breathed the question on a trembling sigh.

"Oh, yes, I really do," he told her gently. There was a distinct lessening of the tension in her body at his teasing tone, and a lifting from her features of the cornered, haunted look she'd worn when he first came in. "As a matter of fact, wouldn't you rather

153

stay here and have an intimate dinner?" he asked in his most suggestive manner.

One corner of Adrian's mouth tensed in annoyance. "No, I would not. I've spent the entire day cleaning and doing the marketing. I'm in the mood to go out to dinner and, later, dancing as well."

"Dear me, Adrian. You sound remarkably like a housewife. But even so, I'll be happy to do as you suggest. Dinner and dancing it will be."

Adrian eyed him suspiciously. "You're being very agreeable, Simon, even if you're taking me out at Jason's insistence, and that always disturbs me. I'd rather see you up to your old tricks than this saintly role you've been striving for lately."

"Don't worry, sweetheart, you'll be back in my bed before much longer," he retorted without batting an eye.

"Why you lecherous, egotistical bastard!" she exploded, her firm breasts heaving with righteous indignation. "I wouldn't . . . you can't . . ."

"Shh." Simon closed the gap between them with two long strides. He caught her to him, his large frame shaking with suppressed laughter at her wrath. "Nice little girls don't swear," he murmured, bending his head until his forehead was resting against hers. He traced the provocative neckline of the sparkling top with one finger and let it nestle in the shadowed cleft between her breasts.

"Si-Simon, please, don't," she whispered, her long lashes sweeping down and hiding the desire burning in her blue orbs. She could feel every hot, hard inch of him from chest to thigh.

154

"Why, Adrian," he murmured reprovingly. His lips moved over her face, dropping light, teasing kisses. "I'm beginning to think I'll have to abduct you."

"That's ridiculous," she said in a shaky voice, her own lips meeting his in reckless response. "An abduction should be mysterious, a surprise. Not blurted out in the presence of the victim."

"Somehow I get the impression my intended victim isn't very alarmed by my threat." He turned his lips to the throbbing pulse in her neck and traced it with the tip of his tongue.

"No," she shuddered, her hands clutching his shoulders. "I know that if you decided to do such a thing, nothing could stop you."

Simon threw back his head and laughed, hugging Adrian in a bone-crushing embrace that threatened to do extensive damage to her ribs. "God, Adrian," he rasped when he was in control again. "You're like a breath of fresh air in my jaded life. I've never met a woman who considered me the perpetrator of so many evil deeds and had the nerve to tell me so to my face. Nor one who could look at me across a crowded room and have me trembling like some young buck on his first date."

Adrian stepped out of the close circle of his arms and walked over to the sofa, where she picked up her small black clutch bag and her jacket in the same fabric as her top.

"You're being very complimentary tonight, Simon," she smiled in an attempt to lighten the mood that all of a sudden had turned far too serious. "I'm more accustomed to dealing with you constantly attempting to intimidate me."

"Am I successful?"

"No, but I'm wary of you just the same."

He took the jacket and held it while she slipped her arms into it. His hands closed over her shoulders, and he turned her to face him. "I always get what I want, Adrian, and I do want you."

"So you've told me before. Since both of us are known for our stubbornness and our tempers, it should prove interesting."

CHAPTER ELEVEN

The restaurant Simon took her to was one of Adrian's favorites. She was a frequent patron, and the maître d's discreet smile of welcome didn't go unnoticed by Simon's alert eye.

As soon as the elderly gentleman had shown them to their table, seated Adrian, and then disappeared, Simon had his say.

"From now on I think we'll eat in. Even that old fool couldn't keep his eyes off you," he remarked darkly.

"Poor Simon," Adrian laughed. "Don't worry, I promise to devote my full attention to you. No matter what you say, I'll pretend to be properly impressed," she teased. "How's that?

"Cheeky wench, aren't you? Pretend, indeed." He regarded her with lazy indulgence. "I'll make you pay for those unkind remarks."

Adrian leaned forward, her eyes gleaming with mischief. "You do not have a sense of humor, Mr. Lord."

His comeback was prevented by the arrival of the waiter.

As the two men spoke in low-voiced conversation, Adrian sat back and let her eyes feast on the rugged sameness of Simon that had become a vital part of her life.

She'd used her strongest weapons in the private war they'd declared on each other, but he was stronger, always ahead of her mapping out the next skirmish.

"Do I have a spot on my nose?" His deep voice brought her back to the present.

Adrian met his laughing gaze across the table, thinking, as she had so many times before, that it was an absolute sin for any man to be as attractive as he was.

"No," she told him. "I was thinking what a blackhearted rake you are." It was crazy, but her earlier moments of panic and uncertainty had turned into an insane recklessness.

Simon leaned forward. "I'm willing to let a certain redheaded witch have carte blanche in reforming me. But for some reason she seems reluctant to take on the job."

"You have it all wrong, Simon." She made no effort to hide the seductive challenge in her eyes. "It's the odds that frighten me. I'm not a gambler."

"Then look on me as a sure thing."

"I might do just that."

One dark, thick brow arched meaningfully. "You talk mighty brave when you know you're safe, don't you?"

"Of course," she grinned. "Isn't that how you do it? I may not be as experienced as you are, but I'm a fast learner."

"Mmm," he muttered darkly. "You're learning too fast to suit me. Since you look upon our relationship as some sort of learning process—your words, not mine—perhaps the next phase will be more exciting." He sat back then, his hooded gaze never leaving her face.

"There's more?" Adrian asked. "I thought we'd done . . . I mean . . ." She floundered helplessly, her face a flaming red. Heavens! she thought wildly. What else can there be about him, especially in the way he makes love?

"There's lots more, Adrian." He continued the embarrassing conversation. "I want to get you all to myself for days and days, maybe even months. I'll hide all your clothes and I'll make love to you morning, noon, and night. Ah, yes," he nodded thoughtfully. "The more I think about it, the better I like the idea."

Adrian could hardly restrain herself from gaping like a fish. "You're insane," she hissed, her eyes darting to the tables nearest them in fear that their ridiculous conversation would be overheard. "You're also a pervert!"

"How did you guess?" he asked unabashed. "My thoughts stay with you constantly, Adrian. I dream of ways of bringing those adorable little purring

159

sounds to your lips when we make love. You'd be surprised at the things you say when you're lying in my arms all quivering and warm with passion."

"Stop it!" she demanded in a frantic voice, and then suffered the indignity of having an elderly couple stare at her. "See what you've done?" She glared furiously at him. "Now they're wondering what sort of weirdos we are."

"I doubt that," Simon chuckled. "The gentleman is probably wishing he had you seated across from him rather than that stern matron he's saddled with. Do you happen to know them?"

"No. And I hope I never see them again," she icily informed him. "You've embarrassed me enough."

"Then why did you start it, Adrian? For you did, you know. From the minute you opened the door to me, you've been flashing signals like a lighthouse."

She lowered her head in confusion. He was right, and it galled her to admit it. It was just that . . . "You don't understand," she eventually managed in a small, hurt voice.

"But I do understand, honey. That's what keeps me coming back to you, keeps me picking away at that shell you've surrounded yourself with." He reached across the table and took her hand. "Even now you're trembling." His fingers curled protectively around her slim ones. "Look at me, Adrian."

With a quiet dread she raised her head and met his dark eyes, almost flinching from the scorching glow that she found there.

"You're going to have to face the future whether

160

you want to or not. And that future doesn't include Jason Lang."

"What if I choose not to?" She uttered the question more out of defiance than anything else.

"Then I'll do it for you," he bluntly informed her. "The brass ring only goes by once in a man's life, honey, and I'll be damned if I'll let your cussed stubbornness wreck both our lives."

"Don't include me in your deceitful games, Simon. I feel bad enough as it is."

"You'll get over it," he remarked coolly. "I was your first lover and I mean to be your last." His voice reminded Adrian of a bell, grimly tolling its message of doom.

"Not unless I say so." She met his flinty stare with her equally determined one.

"Would you care to place a small wager on that, Miss Kohl?"

She didn't answer him because she couldn't. By allowing herself to fall in love with Simon, she felt cornered, boxed in. She'd done the same with Jason, letting their relationship go on, ignoring the warning signs that pointed out his weaknesses, his lack of strength. Now she was caught in a web of pity for him. Wasn't there ever an easy decision when dealing with matters of the heart?

She wanted the tall, powerful man seated across from her. She loved him. But even her love couldn't overlook the fact that to him she was simply another goal, something he saw, liked, and had to have. Adrian had too much pride to give herself to him at any cost.

Conversation was sporadic as their wine, then later, dinner was served. Simon offered no quick fix to end her remorseful attitude, seeming content to let her sort it out for herself.

Adrian watched him surreptitiously from beneath heavily fringed lids, more than a little irked that her unhappiness had so little effect on his appetite. She was about to comment on this fact when she happened to glance past him, her gaze locking with that of Stella Lang's.

"Oh, no!" she exclaimed in a smothered undertone.

"Is something wrong?" Simon asked.

"Stella Lang is coming over. Need I say more?"

"No, but neither should you look guilty as hell," he snapped. "Let me handle Jason's mama."

"Gladly." She smiled through clenched teeth as the person in question drew abreast of their table.

"What an interesting surprise," Stella greeted them, her tiny green eyes darting from one to the other like two small green marbles. "Adrian—how nice to see you," she smiled sweetly. "And Simon. It's good to see you enjoying the food our city is so famous for. How kind of Adrian to take time off from her busy schedule to show you around."

Upon her arrival Simon had pushed back his chair and rose to his feet. If Adrian thought his voice cool earlier, it was frigid as he nodded to Stella and invited her to join them.

"Oh," she twittered, "if you insist. But only for a moment. My friends are waiting for me." She smiled and accepted the chair Simon held. "Tell me, Adrian, have you met the charming young woman Simon has working with Jason?"

"Yes, I have. Janelle is lovely," Adrian quietly replied.

"I'd be a little jealous if I were you," the older woman said. There was a malicious gleam in her eyes and a smug confidence about her. "Jason brought her over for dinner the last time they were home. Oh, dear"—she raised a hand to her mouth—"that just slipped out." She reached over and patted Adrian on the arm. "We did try to call you, dear, but you were out of the office. Could it have been that you were acquainting Simon with our lovely old city?"

"That's very possible, Mrs. Lang. Adrian, with your son's permission, has made my move to Savannah most pleasurable," Simon skillfully parried the cutting remark.

"Really? How nice," Stella murmured, losing some of her effervescence at his reply. She looked coolly at Adrian. "Have you heard from Jason recently?"

"Yes. A couple of nights ago. He's supposed to be in later this evening."

"Well, I must be getting back to my table." She got to her feet. "I'm sure we'll be meeting again."

"Most definitely," Simon agreed as he stood waiting for her to leave.

Stella flashed him her most charming smile, then directed a cool nod to Adrian and swept away, the wretched perfume she wore trailing after her.

"How could you ever think you would be happy

with that bitch hanging around your neck for the rest of your life?" Simon demanded as he sat back down.

"Don't be silly. We knew the first time we met that we'd always be enemies. By the way, exactly what did you say to her regarding that piece of paper she was so proud of?"

"Enough to keep her silenced for life," he said shortly. "Let it drop. She's no threat to you now."

Which Adrian did. Stella Lang was a subject she never wanted to discuss again.

"I think dancing is the next thing on the agenda," he reminded her after signaling for the waiter.

"Why don't we skip it? I'm tired and I think I'd like to go home."

"We're going dancing, Adrian." He held her gaze across the table. "I want to hold you in my arms and feel your body trembling from my touch."

"Why?" The question burst from her lips before she had a chance to think. "You're obviously angry with me, and I'm not exactly thrilled to death with you. Why prolong the agony?"

"I have my reasons," was his curt reply, then he lapsed into a stony silence.

Adrian had never encountered a quiet, brooding Simon, and it baffled her. He held her close in his arms as they danced, letting his hands slide underneath her jacket to graze over the bare skin of her back.

There was a thoughtful narrowing of his eyes, his expression grim. Without knowing why or even stopping to analyze the reasoning behind it, Adrian raised one hand to his face, her palm curving to fit his taut jawline. "Is there a law that says you can't smile?" she murmured, her lips brushing the forceful thrust of his chin.

Simon reached up and caught her hand and threaded his fingers between hers and drew them both to his chest. He looked down at her and smiled. "I'm plotting your downfall."

Adrian sighed, letting her body relax more into the solid firmness of his. Her feet followed his lead unthinkingly. He was an excellent dancer.

"No hysterics?" he breathed against her hair, as one hand snaked down and pressed against her hips, molding her to him in a gesture that set her senses racing.

"Is that what you want?" she managed. The heat of him was reaching out and catching hold of her, seeping into her every pore. His hands moved over her, his fingers working their way up her spine with familiar sureness.

When she stumbled, the solidness of his body cushioned her and his hold tightened. "Am I bothering you?" he rasped, then let his hot tongue tease the soft, pink tip of her ear.

"Yes, damn you!" she admitted. Her eyes were tightly closed as she felt the answering pull of desire stirring in her body. She wanted more than this teasing he was using against her, wanted the long, hard length of his body against hers.

"Then I've succeeded." The cold, hard sound of his voice washed over her. The gist of his words clamped an ice cold sheet over her throbbing body.

"Wha—what did you say?"

He stared down at her, the shadowy dimness adding a cruel twist to his granite features. The music and the faces of the other couples faded as the shock began to hit her.

"I meant for you to respond to me. I planned it this way." There was no fancy wrapping of his words, no softening of the blow. He was blunt and to the point.

Something took hold of Adrian at that moment. She twisted out of his arms and pushed her way through the crowd. Fortunately their table was near the dance floor. She made a grab for her small purse without slowing down. Simon was behind her, but Adrian also knew he'd have to stop and pay their check.

She ran as though the hounds of hell were nipping at her heels, not satisfied until she was on the street. The sight of a waiting taxi was the most beautiful thing she'd ever seen. Without hesitating, she hurried over and grasped the door handle and gave the driver her address.

Once under way, Adrian felt the sharp sting of tears rush to her eyes. Tears of humiliation and shame. *How could I?* she kept repeating over and over in her mind. *How could I ever have let him humiliate me so?*

But the answer was no more palatable than the question. She loved him.

Away from Simon she could function as a sane, normal individual, even to ridiculing the crazy hold he held over her. With him, she became a willing captive, hungering for his touch.

When the taxi stopped in front of her apartment, Adrian thrust a bill toward the driver, then opened the door and fled.

"Hey, lady," the young man called. "You've forgotten your change." When she gave no indication of having heard him, he shrugged and drove off.

Inside her apartment Adrian not only locked the door, she also slipped the chain into place and shot home the dead-bolt lock. There wouldn't be a repeat of Simon's bursting in on her with some flimsy excuse as he'd used last time.

A long shuddering sigh escaped her as she walked through to the bedroom and began to undress. Her movements were lethargic, her heart dulled with pain.

She'd never been one to wallow in self-pity, meeting life and its challenges head-on. But Simon's brutal treatment had wounded her and she was hurting.

As she reached in the closet for a hanger, the glow from the lamp beside her bed caught the gleam of the diamond on her hand. Adrian paused; the hanger and the silvery top fell to the floor.

For the first time since becoming riddled with doubt about Jason, she knew she couldn't marry him. His goodness would grow stale with time and she'd become bored.

With a determined gleam in her eyes she walked over to the walnut dresser, opened a drawer, and took out the tiny velvet box. She removed the ring and placed it into the box and let the lid snap shut.

"If only Simon could be disposed of so easily," she whispered. She folded her arms tight across her breasts, praying for the relief that could come only from crying. But her prayers fell on deaf ears, for nothing more than a brilliant mist blurred her vision. She felt totally and completely alone. She'd gone full circle, had even fleetingly held happiness in the palm of her hand only to see it slip away.

Simon didn't love her; he merely wanted her. All those things she'd read into the looks he'd given her, the fast-paced, confusing conversations they'd had were nothing more than his slick way of drawing her more securely into his net.

He wanted a warm, passionate body, preferably without a face, and certainly without a mind. Adrian could be neither. She needed, no, craved that special gift from someone of belonging to him.

The pounding on her door could be heard faintly above the steady flow of water from the shower, but Adrian ignored it. Apparently he'd been ringing the doorbell as well, but she hadn't heard. She closed her ears to the sound and continued to let the sluice of warm water flow over her.

After several minutes of not moving she reached out and turned off the faucet, then pushed open the shower doors and stepped out. She picked up a thick towel and began drying herself, seeming intent on removing every particle of moisture from her body.

"That's the way," she softly murmured. "Take one thing at a time. That's the only way you'll make it." There was a constriction in her chest, radiating a dull ache for which she had no cure.

She dropped the towel in the wicker basket where she kept her dirty clothes and padded into the bedroom. She took a flannel nightgown from a drawer and put it on, the soft folds bringing her a small measure of comfort.

One last trip was made through the kitchen and living room to assure herself that all windows and doors were locked and the lights were turned off. She went back to the bedroom, got into bed, and turned off the lamp. She never wanted to see Simon Lord again.

Perhaps it was the wine she'd had at dinner, or it could have been exhaustion. But sleep came fast, mercifully relieving Adrian of the pain tearing her apart. The only interruption was the jarring ring of the telephone. After being aroused by the noise two or three times, she let the receiver fall to the floor, refusing to answer the deep voice demanding that she talk to him.

There was a briskness in the air that should have been refreshing to Adrian as she drove along. Her destination, however, took precedence over such mundane things as enjoying the early morning sunrise. There was very little traffic on the streets at the early hour on Sunday morning. On awakening she was still in agreement with the decision she'd made the evening before.

There was a moment of quiet panic when the familiar duplex and its old-brick façade came into view. Adrian drew a deep breath, then parked her car alongside Jason's and got out. She wasn't looking forward to seeing him, but it had to be done. His ring was in her purse, and she was going to return it.

When she reached the front door of Jason's apartment she knocked and waited. If he wasn't home, she planned on leaving the ring with a note. Perhaps a cowardly thing to do, but at least it would be a start.

After waiting what she considered time enough for him to answer, Adrian inserted the key he'd given her months ago and opened the door.

The living room, the furnishings chosen by Stella, was dim, the draperies across the windows still drawn against the morning sun. Odd, she thought as she closed the door behind her, Jason's luggage was standing in the middle of the room. Why hadn't he answered the door?

Dismissing it as unimportant, Adrian tiptoed down the hall to his bedroom. When she reached the door she stretched out her hand . . . then froze.

There were sounds coming from the room, Jason's voice in teasing laughter and the pleased murmur of a woman.

Adrian jerked back her hand as though she'd received some kind of electrical shock. She was surprised, even stunned, but strangely enough she wasn't hurt.

She turned to leave as quietly as she'd entered, when the bedroom door suddenly opened to reveal Jason, wearing only the navy blue bottoms of a pair of pajamas.

When he saw Adrian he reacted like a man who

had been poleaxed. "Adrian!" he got out in stunned disbelief. He reached out to her, then withdrew his hand and ran it over his ashen face. "It's not . . . I mean . . ."

"Don't, Jason," she quietly stopped him. "Don't you think it would be kinder to close the door?" She was almost tempted to laugh at the naked figure of Janelle, frozen in utter stupefaction where she was sitting in the middle of the rumpled bed.

Jason did move then. He jerked the door to, then caught Adrian by the arm and rushed her to the living room. "You've got to let me explain," he began again. His nervousness carried him in aimless pacing across the room. "Janelle and I . . . it's not at all what you're thinking. We got in late, we were both tired . . ." He shook his head. "I honestly can't say how it happened."

"Don't explain, please," Adrian said. She opened her purse and brought out the box that held his ring. "I came over here to bring you this. I've given it a lot of thought, and I can't marry you." She placed the box on the coffee table.

Jason stared in disbelief at the tiny box, then swung his gaze to Adrian. "No wonder you're acting so cool about the whole thing." He gave a short mirthless laugh. "I'm feeling like a heel, and all the while you were waiting to stick a knife in my back."

"That's not the way it is at all, Jason. I wasn't spying on you, and I did have a key." She removed it from her leather key holder and placed it next to the ring. "It seemed only fair that I see you face to face rather than leaving you a note, which is what I was going to do if you hadn't been in."

"So Mother was correct. You have fallen for Simon Lord, haven't you?" he lashed out angrily. There was a sneering expression on his face that for one brief moment reminded Adrian of Stella.

"I have gone out with Simon," she coolly admitted, refusing to be drawn into a fight. "But if you recall, you offered me to him on a silver platter."

"Sure." He sounded ugly. "But his millions made the transition incredibly easy, didn't it, Adrian?"

"Don't you think you're being a trifle ridiculous? After all, your friend is in your bedroom, in your bed, minus her clothes. I really don't think you're in any position to be hurling accusations at me." She turned and walked to the door. "Good-bye, Jason. I wish you every happiness."

There was a lightness to her steps as she walked back to her car and got in. As she edged the VW into the traffic and toward her apartment, Adrian couldn't help but shake her head at the incongruity of the situation. All the while she'd been agonizing over her unfaithfulness to Jason, he'd been snugly ensconced in Janelle's bed.

As much as she hated to admit it, Simon had read Jason like a book. She considered sending Simon some sort of prize, preferably a bomb, for having correctly entered their lives, made his observations and predictions, then placed in motion his destructive plans.

Well, now both men were out of her life. And while there were sure to be moments of painful remembrances, as well as sharp aches that would tear at her heart, Adrian knew she would weather the storm. She had no intention of sitting around brooding.

CHAPTER TWELVE

For all her brave thoughts about facing the future, there was a forlorn look about Adrian's face as she walked with head bent toward her apartment. There was a lonely sound in the hollow ring of her footsteps against the stone flooring.

Her fingers sought and found the key to her door without her even looking. But before she could do more than touch the tiny metal tip of the key against the lock, the door was flung open. A hand shot out and caught her wrist, and jerked her inside.

The muscles of her throat instinctively joined forces and prepared to send forth a bloodcurdling scream from lips parted in readiness. Before the sound could break the early morning stillness, however, Adrian was swung around to face her assailant.

"Where the bloody hell have you been?" demanded a grim-faced Simon. Adrian swallowed convulsively, her initial fear of being assaulted by some maniac taking a back seat to the smoldering rage emanating from the huge man towering over her.

She pushed at the iron grip of the hand that was paralyzing her wrist, and nervously licked lips that had gone dry as cotton. "Ou-out," she squeaked in a high, trembling voice. *My God! He's ready to murder me,* she thought incredulously, and tried to back away.

She'd never seen a human being so consumed with anger. His face was a study of a man having been pushed beyond his endurance. Eyes that had sparkled so devilishly now resembled bottomless black pools of swirling turmoil. His features were locked into such a painful grip of suffering, Adrian could hardly bear to look at him. His mouth resembled a cold, colorless slash across the iced stoniness of his face.

"By God, I know you've been out." Simon finally spoke in a deathly quiet voice that sent shivers of fear up Adrian's spine. "What I want to know is who you were with?"

"Jason." She gave the information without thinking.

Her wrist was released then, but his hands gripped her shoulders instead. "Adrian . . ." he said, his breathing reduced to short, painful gasps. "Did you spend the night with Lang?"

For a moment, in spite of her fear of him in his present mood, Adrian was tempted not to answer, to prolong his agony. He'd hurt her and she wanted her revenge. But the love she felt for this impossible man tugged at her heart. She knew she would never deliberately hurt him.

"No," she said softly. "I went over this morning to return his ring."

Simon gave a groan of relief and crushed her to his chest, his arms molding her to him. "I was about to go out of my mind," he sighed, his lips moving feverishly against her throat.

"I've only been gone for about forty-five minutes," Adrian told him. His heart was thudding at an alarming pace, and she could see a fine film of perspiration on the burnished column of his neck. Alarm shot through her that he might be ill.

"Simon? Are . . . are you all right?" she asked, concerned. Angry or not, she refused to stand by idly and see him suffer.

"No," he grated omniously. "I'm not all right." He raised his head and stared down into her face. "I'm beginning to recuperate, but I'm far from well."

"I wasn't referring to your emotional state, and you know it. I wondered if you are sick. It's cool this morning, but you're perspiring." Adrian forced her voice to be brisk and to the point.

"I'm sweating, you redheaded witch, because I thought I'd driven you into Lang's arms." His hands slipped up to cup her face. "I know I hurt you last night." He gave her a lopsided grin. "But I was only trying to force you to take a long hard look at what you were doing to us. You didn't love Jason, and I knew it."

Adrian very calmly reached up and removed his hands from her face, then stepped back. "Is that all?"

176

she asked pointedly, calling on every ounce of will power she possessed not to be swayed by his beguiling smile and his familiar touch.

"All?" he roared, his brow grooving as he stared at her. "What the hell are you talking about?" he demanded. He took one long step and caught her to him.

"Oh, no." She struggled free and darted around to the other side of the sofa and glowered at him. "Now, Mr. Lord, let me enlighten you to a few home truths about yourself. First, I didn't care to be humiliated in public or in private the way you did to me last night. Second, until you're ready to apologize for your crude behavior, I don't want to see or hear from you. If you find the aforementioned distasteful, then you may consider our brief . . . er . . . encounter as a pleasant passing of time, for that's how I'll remember it."

A deathly silence settled over the room. Simon stared at her as though she'd taken leave of her senses. She watched his eyes, narrowed to thoughtful slits, saw them flicker, silently measuring the distance around the sofa. That was her worst mistake.

"There'll be no apology, Miss Kohl," he replied in a steely voice.

"Then walk."

"Like hell I will."

Before the words were out of his mouth, he'd simply thrown one long leg over the back of the sofa onto the cushioned seat and then was standing beside her. "You were saying?"

"Get out of my apartment, Simon." Adrian was

furious. He'd scoffed at her request for an apology and he'd outsmarted her.

"Not until I've talked some sense into that beautiful but thick head of yours." Without giving her a chance to disagree, he pushed her down on the sofa, then planted himself squarely in front of her on the solid wood of the coffee table.

"Your regard for furniture leaves a lot to be desired," she remarked sarcastically, wearing her injured pride like a mantle about her shoulders. Rather than look at Simon, Adrian let her eyes drop to her hands, which were tightly clenched in her lap.

"I'm not moving, Adrian, so you may as well stop pouting and look at me," Simon chided her gently.

"I can hope," was her stormy reply.

"Will it help if I tell you that I love you?"

It was another trick, and she wasn't about to fall for it. "Am I suppose to jump for joy at hearing those three words, Simon?" She braved the searing gleam in his eyes. "They mean nothing, and you know it. You are a taker. Your whole philosophy is built around taking. Anything that strikes your fancy, even women . . . especially women. Well, you can count me out. I'm not interested in becoming one of your possessions."

Simon reached out and clasped her nape with a warm hand. "The words sound brave, but I don't believe them, Adrian. Perhaps I went about it all wrong, but I knew you weren't meant for Jason. And"—he cocked a dark brow—"you obviously agree. Why else would you have given him back his ring?"

178

"I'd rather not discuss Jason with you," she said frostily. The whole affair was crazy. In less than twenty-four hours, she'd been humiliated by Simon, and had caught Jason in a most compromising situation with Janelle.

"Exactly what happened when you gave Lang back his ring?" Simon asked in a deceptively soft voice. "Did he get ugly?"

Adrian brushed aside his hand and got to her feet. She started toward the kitchen, then paused. "I suppose you'll find out soon enough. As you predicted, Jason was unable to resist Janelle. I quite unintentionally surprised them in his bedroom this morning. When we eventually made it to the living room, I gave him the ring. He retaliated in kind, by accusing me of having fallen for you. So," she said, her voice quivery, "how does it feel to be so damned right, Simon? You've àccomplished all you set out to do. I hope the victory is a sweet one." She turned on her heel and left the room.

Bacon and eggs were brought from the fridge, along with butter and orange juice. With quiet dignity Adrian moved about the small kitchen. Coffee was put on, then strips of bacon placed on a rack and popped beneath the broiler. She was beating bright yellow eggs in a bowl when Simon entered the compact space of the room.

He made no effort to break the stormy silence, seemingly content just to watch Adrian. The only peek she dared risk in his direction revealed no visible signs of remorse in his face. In fact, she concluded acidly, he appeared inordinately pleased with himself.

When it was time for the bacon to come out, she performed the task deftly, laying the crisp, brown strips on paper towels to drain. As she was about to pour the eggs into the waiting skillet, she decided Simon could offer some contribution toward the meal. "You can fix the toast and set the table."

"Yes, ma'am."

Such a meek manner was viewed by Adrian with a suspicious glint in her eye. When Simon became a repentant individual, he was at his deadliest.

"How many pieces for you?" he asked, holding up two pieces of bread.

"One. There's jelly and marmalade in the fridge," she stated coldly.

By the time the eggs were done there was a rack of perfectly browned toast on the table, along with plates, cutlery, and cups and saucers. Adrian divided the eggs into two portions, giving Simon the larger one. The same was done with the bacon.

When they were finally seated, she tried to pretend she was alone, but nothing short of total blindness could blot out the man sitting opposite her. Her brain might send out messages of hate and distrust, but her heart was capable only of loving him.

"How long is the cold war going to continue, Adrian?" he asked her when they were halfway through the meal.

"I'd like to say forever, but I'm sure you'll find a way to change it."

"Red hair is synonymous with a hot temper,

sweetheart, but bad manners don't become you."
There was a gentle tone in his rebuff, also an underlying message that he wouldn't tolerate much more.

Adrian took a deep shuddering breath. "I'm sorry.
I have been rude, and I apologize."

Simon sat back in his chair, admiration visible in
his dark eyes. "Very nicely done, Adrian. Now I
have a question to ask you and I want an honest
answer. Not a rash of wild excuses and accusations.
Okay?"

"I'm not stupid, Simon. I'm capable of answering
a simple question without attacking you," she said
sweetly, the smile on her lips conspicuously absent
from her stormy gaze.

"Will you marry me? Within the week?"

For what seemed like an eternity, but was in reality only a few seconds, Adrian sat staring at him, her
expression turning to one of complete shock.

He leaned forward and waved one hand before her
eyes in a comical gesture of breaking her trance.
"Adrian? Did you hear me?"

She gave a tight nod, her bottom lip caught between her teeth as she stared at him across the table.
"Y-yes, I heard you."

"Well?"

"I don't know, Simon. I honestly wasn't expecting
this," she told him.

Simon frowned. "Honest to the bitter end, aren't
you? You must learn tact, Adrian. My back is practically raw from the tongue-lashings I've taken from
you." He caught the hand that was resting on the
table and held it between both of his. "I love you,

181

Adrian Kohl, and I want to spend the rest of my life making you happy."

Adrian, her senses still swirling, could barely take in what was happening. All the horrid things she'd accused him of came rushing back to haunt her, for never had she expected a proposal of marriage. In fact, she'd done an excellent job of brainwashing herself into believing that marriage was the furthest thing from his mind. Now her future hung in the balance, and she didn't want to face it without Simon.

"Yes, I'll marry you," she said in a voice so soft he could barely hear her.

"Thank you, Adrian. I won't let you down, I promise. Are you through eating?"

"Yes."

"Then let's make use of your sofa. Besides wanting to make love to you, which I fully intend to do, I see far too many questions reflected in those blue eyes."

Moments later Adrian found herself neatly tucked beneath Simon's arm. She could hardly believe that little more than an hour ago she'd vowed never to see him again.

"What prompted you to give Jason's ring back to him?" Simon asked her.

She shrugged. "I knew weeks ago that marriage to Jason was out of the question. Subconsciously, I suppose I was just waiting for an excuse."

"Which turned out to be me," Simon filled in.

"And how. Part of my resistance was due to the atrocious way I thought you were treating Jason."

"Unfortunately, sweetheart, that's the role you've

182

been playing from the beginning. He will always need a woman he can lean on."

"Stella's influence," she softly murmured.

"Who knows? I'm sure it helped, but who can really say? All I was interested in was getting you out of a situation that could only bring you grief." He bent his head and kissed her forehead. "I knew after the Cromiers' party that I had to find a way to get you to myself. After I made love to you, I knew I would find a way."

"The perfect example of a true rake," Adrian murmured, twisting around so that it was her lips and not her forehead that received his kisses. "Mmm . . ." She broke away, a bemused look on her face. "You're an expert at making love, at kissing, turning out salads, toast, a financial genius. Isn't there anything you can't do?"

"Yes," Simon shortly retorted as he pulled her onto his lap. "I'm a miserable failure when it comes to bringing you to heel. Instead of giving you a good spanking, which is what you usually need, all I can think of is grabbing you and taking you to bed."

"That's interesting," Adrian coyly replied, one slender hand finding its way between the buttons of his shirt and teasing the dark tufts of hair on his chest. "That you've had such strong urges to make love to me, that is. It's also been the best kept secret in the world these last few weeks. And"—she gave a short pull to the hair between her thumb and forefinger—"I'll never forget what you said to me last night."

Simon bore his punishment bravely, too bravely to

suit Adrian. She looked up at him and saw desire in his eyes. "I was desperate, Adrian. Jason was due back and I wasn't sure what you would do. Will you let me try to make it up to you?" he whispered

"Oh, I expect you to, my darling, and soon."

"Say that again."

"My darling Simon. I love you so much," she murmured in a trembling voice.

A deep shuddering sigh of satisfaction tore through him as the words fell from her lips. He sat forward, then rose to his towering height with Adrian held tight against his chest.

This time when he stopped at the edge of the bed and slowly let her body slide down the length of his until her feet touched the floor, Adrian knew what it meant to give as well take.

With the new confidence of Simon's love fresh in her thoughts, she was as eager as he was to free their bodies of their clothing. When the last restricting garment floated to the floor, Adrian prolonged the moment when Simon would take her, by letting her hands ride upward over lean narrow hips, her eyes following every line and angle of his body.

There was no shame or embarrassment in her at this brazen act. He belonged to her and she wanted to know him with her body, her eyes, and her hands. He'd taken her once in the dark of night, but this time it was day, and not one part of him was hidden from her adoring eyes.

"As much as I'm enjoying this," Simon rasped, "I'm afraid I can't stand much more." He swooped her up and placed her on the bed, his own hair-covered flesh trapping the sensitive tips of her breasts as he came to her. His hands explored familiar trails over sensitive skin, gently probing and squeezing the softness of Adrian's gleaming breasts, then teasing and stroking her waist, the taut flatness of her stomach, and finally the warm inner softness of her thighs.

His lips became involved as they followed his hands, first one, then the other, till Adrian was clutching at his shoulders, pleading with her body for him to relieve the towering inferno threatening to consume her.

"I want you," she whispered hoarsely, arching her hips toward the magic of his hand.

Simon came to her then, his dark gaze needle-sharp with desire.

Adrian woke to the most delicious feeling of something warm and firm along the entire length of her body. She stretched one slender leg, her toes coming in solid contact with Simon's foot.

She had no trouble recounting the last few hours, nor was she shocked that he was still in bed with her. She snuggled closer, hungry for the nearness of the body and spirit she shared with him.

"You are the most restless female I've ever encountered." His voice sounded from deep among the pillows that almost covered his head.

"Watch it, buster." She sounded ominous. "I'd better be the last female you encounter."

"Don't worry, my beautiful witch, you will be," he assured her. "You were so perfect. The first time we made love was unbelievable. But today"—he raised himself up on one elbow and leaned over her—"was out of this world."

"Did I really please you? I'm not very experienced." Suddenly she became shy. There had been so many women before her. Could she hope to satisfy him?

"I'm not looking for someone to match my record, sweetheart, so stop worrying," he chuckled. "Concentrate on me instead. I'm very possessive."

"I know. You're also pushy, overbearing, and impatient," she teased against the steady thump of his heart.

"Do you want a big wedding?" he asked as he thoughtfully ran his fingers through her hair.

"No."

"Good, for two reasons. I won't be content until you are Mrs. Simon Lord."

"The other reason?"

Simon grinned. "You do want babies, don't you?"

"Oh, yes, several. But . . ." Her voice trailed off as it hit her that she could easily be pregnant at that very moment. "I didn't think."

"I know, princess, but I did." He chuckled. "All the time you were raining fire and brimstone down on my head, I was hoping you were carrying my child. You couldn't have gotten rid of me with dynamite."

"What will people say if we get married so quickly?" she asked worriedly.

"I doubt they'll be surprised. Most of your friends

have guessed by now that we're more than just friends."

"Sandra and David will be pleased."

"We'll ask them to go with us. Would you like that?"

"Yes. Very much." She considered the future for a moment. "Where will we live?"

"Wherever you want. Would you like to stay here?" Simon asked. "You could always snub Stella Lang. Think how sweet your revenge will be."

"Yes . . ." Adrian smiled. "It will be, won't it. You won't mind occasionally running into Jason?" she asked curiously.

"I won the prize, sweetheart, he didn't. Besides, knowing you never loved the man does make a difference."

"Mmm."

Simon ran a possessive hand upward over her gleaming thighs, stopping at her breasts. "What devilment are you plotting?" he whispered as his tongue became involved in teasing her ear in a most erotic manner.

"I'm thinking how I'll handle being manipulated by you." She turned her head and frowned up at him. "What about my business? I'm not going to give it up without a fight."

"Of course not, darling," Simon admitted huskily, his mouth going back to her ear and the throbbing pulse beneath it. "You can have ten thousand businesses. Okay?"

By then his hands were touching her body, awakening the passion that seemed to grow stronger each time they made love. "See"—she tried to keep a stern expression on her face—"you're doing it again."

"I certainly hope so," he chuckled as he dropped light, gentle kisses over face and the inviting tips of her breasts. "And I plan on doing it again and again."

"Simon," she squealed as he suddenly flipped over on his back and drew her on top of him. His large hands cupped her buttocks and pressed her hard against the stirring heat of his thighs. "Be serious."

"Damn, sweetheart, if I get any more serious, I'll have a stroke." He gave a powerful thrust of hips that lifted Adrian as well. "Can't you tell how serious I am?" Then he grinned at the suffusion of color that stained her cheeks. All at once he became still, his gaze alert. "I'd never be foolish enough to demand that you give up everything you've worked so hard to achieve, Adrian. But I hope in time, once the babies start, that you'll make arrangements that will satisfy us both. Is that what you wanted to hear?"

When she didn't answer him, he ran his fingers up and down her spine. "Did you hear me, sweet witch?" The silent pleading of her desire-ridden face excited him to a fever pitch.

"Must you talk so much, Simon?" Her voice, her body was sending out a message he couldn't resist.

"Only with love for you, my sweet angel, only with love for you." He caught her hips and guided her to his burning thighs, showing her with more than mere words how deep was his love for her, a love that would surround and protect her till the end of time.

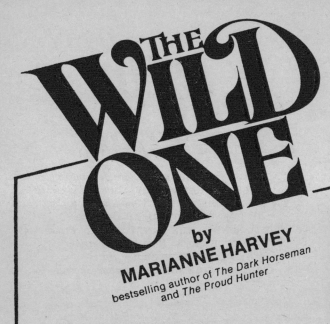

THE WILD ONE

by

MARIANNE HARVEY

bestselling author of *The Dark Horseman*
and *The Proud Hunter*

Proud, beautiful Judith—raised by her stern grandmother on the savage Cornish coast— boldly abandoned herself to one man and sought solace in the arms of another. But only one man could tame her, could match her fiery spirit, could fulfill the passionate promise of rapturous, timeless love.

A Dell Book $2.95   (19207-2)

At your local bookstore or use this handy coupon for ordering:

Seize The Dawn

by Vanessa Royall

For as long as she could remember, Elizabeth Rolfson knew that her destiny lay in America. She arrived in Chicago in 1885, the stunning heiress to a vast empire. As men of daring pressed westward, vying for the land, Elizabeth was swept into the savage struggle. Driven to learn the secret of her past, to find the one man who could still the restlessness of her heart, she would stand alone against the mighty to claim her proud birthright and grasp a dream of undying love. $3.50